ALL THAT SHINES

Also by Ellen Hagan

Don't Call Me a Hurricane
Watch Us Rise (with Renée Watson)
Reckless, Glorious, Girl

ALL THAT SHINES

ELLEN HAGAN

BLOOMSBURY

NEW YORK   LONDON   OXFORD   NEW DELHI   SYDNEY

BLOOMSBURY YA
Bloomsbury Publishing Inc., part of Bloomsbury Publishing Plc
1385 Broadway, New York, NY 10018

BLOOMSBURY and the Diana logo are trademarks of Bloomsbury Publishing Plc

First published in the United States of America in September 2023
by Bloomsbury YA

Bloomsbury books may be purchased for business or promotional use.
For information on bulk purchases please contact Macmillan Corporate and
Premium Sales Department at specialmarkets@macmillan.com

Library of Congress Cataloging-in-Publication Data
available upon request
ISBN 978-1-5476-1021-1 (hardcover) • ISBN 978-1-5476-1022-8 (e-book)

Book design by Jeanette Levy
Typeset by Westchester Publishing Services
Printed and bound in the U.S.A.
2 4 6 8 10 9 7 5 3 1

To find out more about our authors and books visit
www.bloomsbury.com and sign up for our newsletters.

For my parents, who taught me to love who I am &
where I come from. Who raised me on stories of growing up &
always coming home.

Thank you forever to the Bluegrass. Kentucky.
For the stories that don't always get told. For the land.
For corn bread. For rolling hills & cast-iron skillets.
For homecomings. For always dreaming of returning.

HAVING IT ALL

Tonight, We Shine

"Mom, can I borrow your earrings?
The diamonds? I think they'd match,"
I say, twirling, my new dress
swinging just above my knees.
And throwing myself back onto her chaise.

"Of course. Just check in my closet.
But you're almost ready, right?
Because this night is official
and important to me, to your dad.
The biggest evening of our lives.
And your father has been under
such pressure. This is his business,
his everything. Just . . . we need
you to be there and to be your
energetic and true, beautiful self.
Can you do that for us?"

I nod as I take in their dressing room,
the gowns stretched out on chairs
and over couches. Both of us
trying to figure out the exact
combination of perfection.

A Night to Celebrate

Clark Brooks. Dad.
His company. His people.
His community.

All with the family that loves him,
adores him, would do anything
for him. My mom pulls me up,
up and into a hug.

The full-length mirror holds us,
our reflection pointed back.

"Chloe, this is our night," she says.
"A night to celebrate your father
and all of his incredible success.
Everything he has built up
around us. For us."

And I believe every word.

Luxury Over Everything

Our life is big here.
Maxed out. Everything massive
and breaking out at the seams.
And Dad is the biggest of all.
Big personality, big energy,
big life, big performer,
big spirit, big, broad shoulders,
big mood swings, big heart,
big anger, big boisterous joy,
big vacations, big gifts,
big surprises, big gestures,
big meals, big appetite for life,
big smile, but most of all,
big spender.

Showcase

"Hello out there!" Dad yells toward their room.
"The car is here. Let's go! We can't be late.
Come on," he calls up again,
his voice booming.

I look at him across the room.
Dad is our everything.
He looks like a star too.
Tuxedo, black hair perfect.
He is checking his watch
and catches me staring.

"Chloe, you look stunning," he says.
I trust him.
Hold close to every single word.

Mom walks out into the hallway.
She is shimmering too. Long gown.
Diamonds. Everything feels sparkling.
Like gold. Tonight, we glow.

Shine

"Lana, I have something for you."

"There is nothing I want," Mom says,
her smile reaching across the foyer.
The lights twirling outside,
the almost-summer evening sky.
"Just you. Just this family. Just tonight."

"In case you change your mind . . . this is for you,"
he says, handing over a narrow box.
Her smile gleams, stretches even farther
across the room. I know that look.
The one that loves how big he is.
The one that adores his over the top,
his extra, his extravagance. His glitter
and shine. He pulls another identical box
from the bag he is carrying. Inside them
are matching diamond necklaces.
One for Mom
and one for me.

Everything is a production.
He places them around our necks.
The weight heavy and cool.
This moment not letting us down.
We hold onto one another,
this night,
this event
a kind of forever
together.

"For the way you all shine.
For the way you make me shine.
I love you all. Endlessly.
Let's go. The car is waiting."

The Scenic Route

Trees reaching and pushing toward sky.
Everything in full bloom.
Green everywhere.
The grass and leaves all bursting with it.
As far as you can see.
And blue, blue skies.
No clouds, just blue forever.
Against all that green.
And the black painted fences
that stretch and stretch
and line the one-lane highway that leads
from our home out and into town.
The rolling, rolling hills lead up and away
from everything we know.
The trees stretching high above us.
Bluegrass in the distance
and everywhere in front of us.
"To smell Kentucky air is to know God,"
my father is all the time saying.
"To know Kentucky soil,
have it land beneath your fingernails,
is to know what is holy."
Even though Dad has never
had his hands anywhere
near that dirt. Wealthy all his life.
Never mind all that.
This holy, holy landscape
is home to me.
The only one
I have ever known.
The one I will return to.
Always.

Lexington, Kentucky

A town built on excess
and promises, horse farms
and bourbon barrels lined up
in the distance. Alcohol and money.
Horse racing and mint juleps
and figuring out all the ways to win.
Stories and fables told over and over.
Wealth passed down like fine china.
Stays in the family. Handed down
from generation to generation.
Held close around white-cloth-
covered dining tables. Dressed
with silverware and loads of lilies,
hydrangeas, and pink roses
that double up and over themselves
create a kind of collage of flowering,
flowing and smells that take you back
and lead you home. This place
has always been a kind of fairy tale land
to me and my family and friends.
A kind of everything
as long as you have everything.
And we do. Have it all.
My father makes sure we know that
and are thankful for that
and celebrate and honor that.
His whole journey has been to hold up
what he loves most.
And what he loves most
is us.

Always Make an Entrance

We arrive and, as if on cue,
the whole ballroom looks toward him.
He is the one being celebrated.
He is the one on display, being honored.
His star turn. His event. His night.

All of it feels electrified.
Everyone hugging,
clapping him on the shoulder,
telling him he changed their lives.
How much he means to them.
His vision for the company.

Brooks Bourbon Distillery
        Winning.

Brooks Hotels
        Winning.

Brooks Apartment Complexes
        Winning.

Brooks Horse Farms
        Winning.

Brooks Racehorses
        Winning.

His name in lights all over town.
Lexington is his home and throne.
His success. His work. Work.

Work. Work. Always he is working.

Leaving them hungry
for more.

And Leaving Us Wanting More Too

The people who work
for him love him.
This is clear
in the way
he moves
from one crowd
to the next. Pulled
and carried from conversation
to conversation. Laughing,
clapping shoulders, air-kissing,
and asking about families,
remembering every detail.
To them, he is admired
and prized. Respected
and treasured for his sense
of business, for his esteem,
his popularity in the newspapers
and in the social circles
he's been climbing for decades.
But sometimes to us
he is a hologram.
Someone we see
but spend no actual
time with.
Disappeared
in his work
and his spotlight.
But when he talks,
when he commands
attention and gets the room
all watching and studying him,
it is all about us.

The Speech

"Good evening.
Thank you, thank you,
please have a seat.
You are too kind.
This night means everything
to me. My family.
A celebration of decades
of hard work. Finally
paying off. Making my mark.
And to have my beloved wife, Lana,
and my cherished daughter, Chloe,
right here beside me means
the world. You all represent
my whole heart. And you all,"
he gestures to the crowd
all hanging on his every word,
"helped me to make this happen.
You have continued to make sure
that the spotlight is not just on me,
but on us. It is not just mine,
but ours," he says,
bringing me and Mom in for a hug,
to show us off, make it known
we are part of his image,
what he wants
everyone
to see.

The crowd is on their feet,
applauding and whistling,
cheering and hollering.

They love him. Stomping
and clapping, he makes us all
believe everything he says.

My father spins us around

until we are dizzy.
Tipsy on the dance floor
from the endless pours
of champagne.
In this world
there are no rules.
This is what I know
for sure. Toasting
and celebrating.
Speeches and cheers.
A nonstop loop
of success. And my dad
right there
at the center
of it all.

Declan and Lily Arrive

Boyfriend and best friend.
They show up shining too.
Tuxedo and cocktail dress.
Black tie. Ready to party
and celebrate with me.
Our families close,
in business, in pleasure.
We've known each other
since childhood. Together.
Best Dressed Awards.
Most Glowing Personalities.
Most Beautiful.
Most Stunning.
Richest.
Wealthiest.
Have It All.

The Photos Are Ours

The photo booth alive
with our faces.
Declan kisses my cheek,
then neck,
then mouth.
And all of me feels
energized, alive, loved.
So loved I am giddy.

Dance Floor = Ours Too

So we take it over.
This is what it feels like
to have it all.

It is the last days of May.
End of the school year
of what feels like
the best one of my life.
Headed into summer
before senior year
and all I can feel is love,
is everlasting,
is shining,
is just like
everything
I ever wanted
is right here
waiting.

And I can see
the future.
Family,
this love,
on stage.
What matters
most.
Music,
my voice
growing
louder,
getting

stronger,
everyone
seeing
how
we

exist.

Seeing

me.

Spotlight

Suddenly, I get pulled up
onstage to toast, to sing,
to share in the flash of light
too. So I do. Take the mic
and sit at the piano. A song
that has been running all over
my mind. Lyrics fresh and new.

"Dad, Mom, I love you. Thank you.
This is just something I'm working on.
For you both. For this night."

You are my star, you are the sun,
you are my guide, you are the one.

You are my home, never alone,
you are the song I bring along.

So I . . . I wanna tell you I do,
I wanna thank you it's true.

I've got this love in my hands
and I will never let go . . . no, no.

My voice sounds clear,
still small sometimes,
but working to make it
bigger, more powerful,
the words too,
closer to who I am,
what I want to say.

I sing out. So when the applause
reaches me, my smile stretches
for what feels like
forever.

Crowds Surround Me

They congratulate me too.
Talk about summer,
my plans, the future.
They ask about recording,
making an album,
going on tour.
They want to know
where they can see me,
if they can have an autograph
before I become a star.

I know it's just because of him,
but I take it in just the same.
Music is story, is home,
is how I want to tell it.

"Time to celebrate you!"
Declan calls out, even though
this is the first song he's ever
heard me sing. He wants me
for show. I know this,
but play along.

Because I want to show off too.

Tipsy

"Where is the waitress?" Lily calls out,
stomping her high-heeled shoes
and standing up—unsteady
and loud.

"More champagne," I shout, holding
my glass to the sky. Declan leans in.
Smells the back of my neck.

"Let's get out of here," he says,
flashes that smile that's had me
from the beginning. Slick. Smooth.
A little over-the-top. Always.
Just the way I like it.

"No! Not until I get what I want,"
I holler back.
And I always get what I want.

The band is playing
so loud I can't hear myself think.
"Come on!" I pull them both up
and we rush the dance floor.
Phone out, pictures snapped,
pushing our way to the bar.
None of us are known to wait
for what we deserve,
for what we believe
is ours.

Declan pulls me close—closer

tells me he wants me
and he's been waiting
too long. I laugh
because we're still
just getting to know
each other in this way,
because it's new,
because this night
feels like everything
and everyone I know
coming together.
Perfection.

I kiss him long
and steady. "Stay here!
I'm going to get us more,"
I say, tipping my empty glass
up to my mouth.

"This night is ours
and we are everything,"
I call back,
because it is.

Because we are.

At the bar

the line is long, so I pull my phone out,
start to post photos with hashtags

#FamilyBusiness #BlessedBeyond
#Crown #KentuckyRoyalty
#Bourbon #RunForTheRoses #Always

"No wonder he had to put on this big show,
especially with all the drama with his businesses.
You know everything is not always what it seems."

I look up, hear two voices right in front of me
tearing our perfect night apart.

"And did you see Lana and Chloe tonight?
Always over-the-top. And those diamonds?
Come on. How hard do they have to try?"

The women laugh. Their perfume
spills out behind them. Smelling of flowers
and sickly sweet something. Cinnamon,
cloves. I shake my head, shift them away.

Not about to let some jealous society wannabes
mess with my good time, I tell the bartender
to pour me another glass. And to go ahead
and give me the bottle. Tell her my name.
Chloe Brooks.

Make sure to say I am the daughter.

Legacy.

Make sure they all
remember
who I am.

After Midnight

Our driver picks us up.
Mom and me still giddy.
All piled beside Dad
in the back seat, windows down.
We drive from downtown Lexington
to our house just outside of city limits.
The Kentucky country roads quiet
and winding all around me.
My junior year almost done
and about to go away to Europe
for a month this summer
and two weeks studying music in Los Angeles.
My dreams—all of them—feel so close.
I hold on to my father's arm
and rest my head on his shoulder.
Try and clear away what I heard
and any drama trying to weave its way
into our lives. Stay steady in my dreaming.
Mom laces her fingers through mine
and we whirl through all the streets
that lead us home.

Lily texts

Epic Night
Unstoppable
Send pix!
Soooo drunk

Tlk tmrrw

Declan texts

You looked so hot tonight
Love you
Miss you already
Call me when home

I text

More soon
Pix tmrrw
Dead tired
Love y'all
Endless!

Thankful

for Clark Brooks. Dad.
Entrepreneur. Businessman.
Family man. Everything to us.

We celebrate
his sense of pride,
over-the-top
moving mind,
the way his brain
works and works.
His steadiness,
commitment
to work and family.
His show-off
confidence,
cool
charm.
His larger-than-life
love of luxury,
taste,
style,
sense of belonging.
His passion for food,
nights out,
spotlight on.
His love of the land
and home.
His dedication
to the people
who have made him
everything he is.

I look to him
as my guide.
The person
showing me
the way.

One Week from Now

Liftoff. Life rising.
Rushing the world alone.
Own dreams of stages,
applause. Lush life
opening up. Traveling
the whole globe. Showing
exactly who I am. Who
I am meant to be.
Starshine. Glow.
Making music,
and a name for myself.
In lights. In love.
This is the moment
everything changes.
The time to show up
exactly the way
I am meant to.

Before Sleep

Write down all I am thankful for.

1. The arms of everyone I love
   holding tight around me. Thread.
   Braid. How they lift and shape me.

2. The smell of sour mash in the air,
   Kentucky riding shotgun. My hair
   wild and loose in the wind.

3. Glow of the spotlight. Just right.

4. Closing my eyes and seeing
   the future. Performing.
   Singing. Writing.
   On stage.
   Believing.

5. Mom and Dad who trust
   in me. Support me. Help me
   to get where I want to go.

6. Declan and the way his mouth
   feels on mine. Sweet. Surrender.

7. Dancing all night with Lily
   until I had to throw my shoes
   to the side. Every move,
   every moment. The music
   lifting us.

8. Every Kentucky highway
   that leads me home.

Life, Disrupted

Knocking on the door
wakes me.
Pounding.
Crashing.
Sounds of alarm.
They ring over and over.
Fast and in succession.

Who is here so early in the morning?

Normally I'd think: a gift.
Someone congratulating my dad,
us, our family. Someone
sharing something good
from the news, the paper,
something shown on television.

Boom. Boom. Boom.

Pull my hair into a ponytail,
run out to the front door.
Don't want to miss this.

The house smells of fresh flowers.
Peonies everywhere.
The whole downstairs
is fuchsia and pink and blooming.

But I feel chaos and commotion
all around us. Confusion.
I am lost.

"Who is it?" I call out.

Still smiling.

Content.

Satisfied.

The Cops at Our Door

I see Dad still in his pajamas and robe.
Mom standing close.
Always right beside him.

"Sir, please step outside,"
the officer outside of the door says.

The words: "investigation,"
"falsification," "illicit,"
"misrepresentation,"
all get thrown around.

My father is being served.
My father is under investigation.
My father is a fraud.
These accusations
shouted at us.
All of a sudden,
my father
does not exist
the same way
I imagined he did.

The police outside our home.
The police coming to take away
everything I've ever known.

Dad looks over at me.
And it is a face
I do not recognize.
One I have not seen before.

And then he does what is asked of him.
And he disappears right in front of us.

Mom is calling out,
asking for answers,
weeping too,
the kind you do
when you're losing
all you've ever known.

There Is a Before and After

The moment right before this
I could breathe.
Seconds ago it felt like
the beginning of my whole life.
Everything laid out around me.
Precipice is the right word.
At the edge.

And I didn't even know it.

Those were minutes ticking down
just before the explosion.
The instant that everything
you thought you knew was a lie.

"What happened?"

I start with the question
I do not want to be asked myself.
Panic and alarm setting in.

Mom hands over her phone
and I see Dad's smiling face
reflected back to me. Sickness
spreading through my chest.
Photographs from last night.
All of us laughing. All teeth
and perfect grins. Gold. Diamonds.
The way we are all glittering
makes me nauseous.

And then these sentences and words
standing out all around me.

"Accused of criminal fraud . . ."
"Will be prosecuted by the state government . . ."
"Husband and father . . ."
"Been stealing funds from his company for years . . ."
"Bankrupt . . ."
"Loss of personal property . . ."
"Faces conviction . . . illegal activity . . . prison time . . ."

Fraud | Noun

All of a sudden,
I can feel the spiral.
Heart reckless
and body numb.

I think about the definition
of fraud
and everything around me
begins to buzz.

An act of deceiving
or misrepresenting.
A person (my dad) who is not
what he pretends to be.
A cheat.
One who is not
what he
was represented as.
A lie.
Trick.
Sham.
Fake.
Counterfeit.
Imposter.
Passing off
as something
you're not.
Fraudulent.
Double-dealer.
Hustler.
Scam artist.
Swindler.

No Secret

"My god, Chloe,"
Mom says suddenly,
pulling me into a hug. Holding me.
The two of us, alone. Empty.
This is how our home feels.
My chest too.
Out of breath.

I feel the phone buzzing in my hand
and look down. Start to panic and turn it off.
I do not want the endless texts and check-ins.
I do not want the *How are you? Are you okay?*
The *I am so sorry* and especially the *What happened?*

Because I do not know the answers to any of it.
Because my father was just arrested in front of me.
Because I am afraid to find out the truth.
Because I am as scared as Mom
and as lost as Dad, who has disappeared
in an instant. How quickly
your whole life can change.
Be disrupted. Fall apart.

Clark Brooks

has made a mistake
or worse . . . he is a liar.
Has been committing
fraud in his businesses.
Stealing from his life's work
and from the people
and places that have lifted
him up. Wrecking
everything in his path.
Making our life
feel like the end
of the world.

Crowds Surround Us

Our yard goes from silence
to mob scene in under an hour.
We disconnect the phone
which is suddenly ringing
and ringing and ringing.
My ears go numb,
Mom disappears
downstairs with her assistant
and her lawyer and the chef,
who is still making the house
smell like bacon and coffee,
and I have no idea
who we even are
anymore.

Outside my bedroom window
there are two vans
and nosy TV crews
with microphones
and news reporters
who are taking down
our whole life.

Do I even exist?
Shut the blinds,
lock the door,
avoid the mirror,
cry, scream
into my pillow,
catch my breath,

try to breathe,
slow the beating
of my heart.

How to Survive

Silence my brain.
Silence the anxiety.
Silence the heartache.
Silence the doubt.
Silence my friends
and their endless text chains.
Silence all social media.
Silence the newsfeed.
Silence the shame.
Silence my heart
erupting in my chest.
Silence my lungs
about to collapse.
Silence Dad's voice
and his all-the-time
confident and strong.
Silence his lies.
Silence his forever
celebrations of success.
Silence his success.
Silence the house
with all the help
busy inside of it.
The chefs and gardeners,
the drivers and cleaners,
the assistants and dog walkers.
Silence the trash
of my life
piling up
beside me.

All of it
goes quiet.
Silent.
Silent.
Still.

Who Am I Without All That Noise?

Try not to think about my father
and the possibility of prison, or worse,
him hurting himself and disappearing altogether.
I see my childhood, the one that sits untouched
in the back of my mind. Crystallized. Clear.

Look around the bedroom. A place of safety
and beauty. Was any of this real?
Or was it all fake? I stare out and it feels like
I am looking into some fun house mirror
where everything being shown back to me
is distorted and out of shape.

I am looking at one thing and the reality
is something totally and completely different.
That's why I need some type of noise
to block out all this panic happening
inside of me. Put my headphones on
and disappear.

Night Falls

Our yard goes quiet
and everyone
who works for us
leaves.
Goes to their own
homes and families.
Sometimes it is easy
to forget that the people
who work for you
do not love you
like their own.
The nannies
are not your mother.
The drivers
are not your father.
The chefs
not your aunts and uncles.
None of them blood.
The vans pull away
and it's just Mom
and me.
Staring
at each other.

"What now?" she asks.

I want to remind her
that I am the child
in this situation
and have none
of the answers.

But truth is
she is as lost
as I am.

It's Over

In one day, our life implodes.
Detonates itself. Explodes.

Blowing all the way up. I can see it
shred and bend away from me.

This is not the life I am used to,
not the one I am accustomed to.

All it takes are just minutes
for everything I know to evaporate.

And instead of talking, I go on
and hold my mom beside me.

We cry into each other's arms
and I can feel the weight of her.

Whispers his name: "Clark Brooks."
Says it whole over and again.

She is trying to discover who it is
she married. And I can see Dad.

So clearly, he is here. Trying to hold
everything together for us. Façade.

See the fantasy he was keeping steady.
Clark Brooks—owner, manager.

Clark Brooks—genius. Business
savvy. CEO. Forever boss. Titan.

Clark Brooks—let it all slip away.
What will we be left with now?

LEAVING IT ALL BEHIND

Next Morning

Our lawyer is back
talking about deals
and schemes
and get out of jail
for free. But this
is not a game
to anyone anymore.

The phone rings
and it is Dad
on the other end.
His voice distant,
garbled. Confused.
Acting as if
this is normal,
nothing happened,
casual, cool.
Infuriating.

Mom puts us all
on speakerphone
and I want to reach
out and hold him
now too. An only child,
I feel lost and alone.
But still want to protect
him and our history,
his legacy that is all
but disappearing.

Don't Cry

"Lana, honey . . . come on.
People make and lose money
all the time," my dad says,
trying to shove it off.

Pretending this is all a game.
That money, that wealth
can be held or let go of.
So easily. Like this
means nothing to him.

"Just tell the truth,"
my mom shouts into the phone.

There is silence. And then this.

"Months ago, I thought
I'd have to end my life
to protect you all," Dad says
finally.

At this, Mom doubles over,
sees me, and pulls me close.

"That's the kind of trouble
I was in. The kind I'm still in.
The kind that wrecks you.
And now I don't know
how to save us."

How much do my friends know?
What will happen now?
Will everything I'm used to disappear?
What will be left behind?
Who will I be with nothing left?

The words: "bankrupt" and "death"
stay looped and linking in my head.
Could have. Would have.
Now that I know the truth,
will it be enough
to make me think
of ending my life
too?

The House Goes Silent

Empty of the people
who work to make us glow.

We have news from jail:
"flight risk . . . denied bail . . ."
My father is not returning.

Not anytime soon. Mom
disappears to her lawyer
to figure out what's next.

My father's presence all over
from the kitchen to the bar
but in reality, completely gone.

So it's just me. Seventeen years
of an existence I thought
I knew.

Awake alone. Nothing beside me,
no one to comfort me. Nothing.
Hollow. A state I know well.

Make breakfast. Take it all in.
The suddenly warm Kentucky
sunshine. The state of shock.

Our home feels massive
and lonely. Feels empty
of all the warmth.

So I sit staring into morning.
Trying to figure out
how to exist.

"We're leaving too"

Mom looks dead at me.
An announcement.

"We're not staying here."
That simple. That fast.

"What are you talking about?
I'm not . . . we're not leaving."

"We're not staying. End of story,"
she states. As if it's already over.

"Mom, that is totally unhinged,
okay? It's just wrong. No, no!"

She moves from my bedroom
to hers. Over and over. Packs.

Beyond listening to me. Already
silent and shaking. Nerves shooting.

"Mom. We can stay here.
Just wait it out. Come on. Breathe."

"Do you actually think they will let
us keep this house? Chloe? Be real."

I look around. Realize she is right.
All this excess. All this stuff.

This whole existence feels cluttered,
crowded, chaotic. Want to break free.

"Soon enough there will be nothing left.
I don't want to watch it all slip away."

Thin Air

In one weekend, our lives
are ruined. Taken all the way apart.
There is no saving face or grace
or getting over it. There is no
returning to what once was.
No normal. No back to the old days.
There are no more old days.
There is no more normal.
Our home isn't ours anymore.
Or the stuff in it.
Our suitcases get packed so fast
I forget anything was ours
in the first place. Just junk
all of a sudden. Just material
and stuff. Just extra everywhere.
And nothing we can take,
because nothing is ours
anymore.

All we have
is ourselves.

What Money Can Do

Make you feel invincible.

What No Money Can Do

Make you feel invisible.

Going Home

"The Limestone Apartments are ours.
We lived there from the time I was born.
Grew up my whole life there, so I know it well.
And it's still in my name,
so we're going home."
She looks at me now, holding onto her past.
"Remember, your papaw was the super.
The best damn super in the Bluegrass."

I know this story. Have been told it before.
Mom coming from nothing. Pulling herself up.
Bootstraps and all. Her mom and dad
working hard, to the bone. Papaw the super.
Granny cleaning houses. Saving every penny
to put Mom through college. University of Kentucky
where she'd meet the famous Clark Brooks,
who changed everything for her, brought her
out of poverty. The two of them investing,
managing, building together until they got more
and more and more. He gave her everything
she could ever imagine . . . before taking it all away.

Granny and Papaw are long gone. Both passed on
when I was small and we have been left
without a connection to the past.
To what they carried with them.

"That's it. It's time for me, for us, to go home."

What Will You Take with You?

This is the question circling in my mind.
Two suitcases. A whole lifetime.
Seventeen years of collecting.

Pack journals full of poems and songs.
Pack notebooks and favorite pens
that glide smooth across the page.

Guitar. Music books. Recordings
on my phone. Beats. Rhythms.
That's all that matters now.

Favorite dresses. Two pairs of shoes.
Somehow with Dad locked up
none of the stuff even matters.

We drive away

and everything,
all of it,
already feels over,
distant.
Like some long goodbye.
I hold my arm out the window
as Mom swerves and cries.
No answers feel like the right ones.
Both of us in a kind of distant haze.
Mind jumbled.
Broken in on.
Tumbled away from me.
Like some reverse or rewind.
We watch our whole life
dissolve outside the rearview.
Some kind of movie
of what once was.
Goodbye to all that.

Rewind

I think.
I would like
my life back
as the country scenery
evaporates,
and my history
along with it.
We ride
from home,
into the city.
Through downtown
and all the shops
and restaurants
and cafés, the bars,
the bookstores
and offices,
and keep driving
out to the other side
of town.
We see country again.
This place suddenly
as different as you can get.

This Part of Town

It's the part we never go to.

The part that I've been told

is the rough section.

The dangerous part,

whatever that means.

Like there's a line

that divides the *more*

from the *less*.

The excess

from the nothing.

The too much

from the not enough.

Keep My Eyes Open

The Bluegrass looks the same.
All the hilltops and rolling views
out my window. We drive.
Out on to the other side of downtown.
The forgotten and left behind.
The side we've all been warned about.
The side we own
but were always too scared to travel to.
This is our home now.

ime ton Ap tmen s

But when we pull in,
the sign doesn't say
"Limestone," because six
of the letters are missing.
No Limestone.
No Apartments.

Run-down and falling
all apart. We can see it.

"Wait, is this it?" I ask,
rolling the window down.
"This can't be it. Is it?"

Mom nods. It is.
The first property
inherited twenty years ago.
A place to start their wealth,
and the only property in her name.
The only asset we get to keep.

But clearly this place,
once so close to their hearts,
so essential to their work
and growing their business,
has been abandoned.
Let go of.
Shutters loose on windows,
the grass left unmowed,
nothing blooming
or growing.

Just an empty lot.
Trashed and rough
around the edges.
Not at all
like the house
we just left behind.

Limestone

Sedimentary Rock
>What this town is built on,
>the name of this neighborhood too.

Calcite or Aragonite
>Defined by Mom and Dad
>as the other side of town.

Contains Magnesium Carbonate.
>Limestone. Kept away from us,
>shoved and pushed to the side.

Clay, Iron Carbonate
>Spot Mom was born and raised,
>place she kept me away from.

Feldspar, Pyrite, Quartz
>Who do I believe now that I'm here?
>Who can I trust? Not Mom. Not me.

We park

and get a better look around.
Try not to judge or look too close.
There are picnic tables set to the side
and rough-looking grill stations,
a few lawn games set out, and one
rusty old swing set. *Where are we?*
And how could my parents
let this get so bad? Let it go for so long?

Late afternoon and there's a group of kids
sprawled out on one of the tables.
They look to be my age.
Try not to stare too hard.
One of the kids raises his hand
like he's about to ask a question,
or like he already has the answer.
I can't tell, but either way, I don't like it.

"Y'all just moving in or something?"

he asks, holds his palm over his eyes,
blocking the sun shining through.

Mom pops the trunk of the car,
and I start to pull suitcases and duffel bags,
and the truth is, we didn't take much.
We couldn't. And even if we did,
where would it all fit?

I squint back at him and his friends and Mom nods.
Announces her name like they should know
who she is. "Name's Brooks. Lana Brooks.
So good to meet you all. We are in . . ."
she looks down at the scrap of paper
in her hand, "apartment five. Uhh . . .
Can one of you help us find that
and give us a hand too?"

The kid with the raised arm tilts his head.
Another one sighs loud enough for us
to hear, and the other two keep their heads down.

"Sure. I got you. Name's Clint," he says,
reaches out to shake my mom's hand,
but she's already ahead of him.

"There's more bags in there too," she calls.

"Be careful with them," I snap,
knowing I don't want anything to happen
to our last remaining items. Clothes,

keepsakes, heirlooms. And I have no idea
who this person grabbing all
our precious items even is.

"Excuse me?"

a girl says from the picnic table.
Her face says she is over this, over me, already.
"I don't know who you are,
but this is not the Four Seasons
or some fancy resort. This is not
a vacation you're just dropping in on."

"Oh no, I didn't mean . . ." I start.

"Clint is not your valet.
And we do not work for you,"
she keeps on, looking at me
dead in the eyes. I shift, start to sweat.

"Skye, it's cool. I can help.
It's all good. I was bored
sitting around here anyway.
Nice to meet someone new."
Clint looks directly at me.

"No, they should know
that we are not their staff
or their servers.
We live here too.
Same as you two.
We're not here for you.
We're here *with* you.
This is our home.
Welcome to Limestone."

Mom brushes it off.
Hands Clint the bags.
I cringe, realize I didn't even think twice
about telling them what to do
and where to go and how to help.
My face is flush with shame.

That's It

We're gonna die here.
With our jerky ways.
Oh, can you get that bag?
And, oh, could you make sure to . . .

It dawns on me suddenly.
This is real. We are really broke.
My mother has really lost her good sense
and neither of us have any idea
how to act outside of our gated
community and worlds. Sheltered.
Kept away from everyone else.

We are so screwed here. So, so screwed.
Who is coming to save us? To help us?
To cook and clean and manage us?
How are we supposed to survive all of this?
I look around, but have no idea
what that means, or how in the world
we will make that happen.

Unpack

The two of us,
moving around each other,
bumping and navigating.
We haven't been this connected
in such a long stretch of time,
in this close a proximity.
Mom keeps pretending
to know how to clean
and to know her way
around the kitchen.
The food she bought
makes zero sense
and none of it seems edible
without an in-house chef,
which we do not have
anymore. Everything
is out of reach.
And suddenly it's just us.
The two of us.
Connected but distant.
There is no central air
and it is already eighty-five degrees
with Kentucky summer
around the corner.
Needless to say, it is hot
and getting hotter.
The panic is rising
in both of us. We sit
staring out the window
into nothing.

Finally Face It

Turn my phone on
and it begins to buzz
and chime. Messages
completely full. Texts
and missed calls.

As if all of Lexington
has been trying to find
out the scoop. Gossip.
How my family lost
it all in one weekend.

Cut on the television
and it's all over local news.
Brooks Family Disaster.
Brooks Family Fraud.
Brooks Family Tragedy.

Each title feels like the end.
Our lives strewn across
the papers too. The word
"family" making me
an accomplice.

Fifteen missed calls

from Declan alone.
I listen to each message.

"Chloe. Last night
was SICK! Let's hang
this weekend. Call me."

"Party again—tonight?"

"Declan again. You there?"

"Baby. You okay?
You drink too much?"

"Hey. Been hearing things
and starting to get worried.
Call me back when you can."

"Chloe, what's going on?
You're not returning calls
or texts. What is up?"

"I'm coming over.
On my way. We gotta talk."

"I'm here. This is messed up.
You ignoring it is making it worse."

"I'm parked IN YOUR DRIVEWAY!
TV crews trying to block me. What the hell?!"

"Answer the door!
You're just gonna ignore me like that?"

"Chloe. I talked to Lily.
We gotta meet up. Come on."

"Your dad's not the only one
going down for all this."

"People are pissed. You're just
gonna disappear? Ghost us like this?"

"Don't do this Chloe. Answer the phone!"

"I'm done."

Death Threats

Mom's phone a time bomb
of people whose lives
are getting taken down
along with ours. People
whose money is or was tied up
in businesses that my dad
created. Their retirement
and their wealth built up
over time is wasted away
because of us. But
they are not sitting in jail.
At least they are not waiting
on bail that is set too high,
that will not get them out.
They are not removed
from everything they know.
They will survive.
We might not.

Now, I keep asking myself,
what is my worth
now that all my money
is gone?

"I'm not going back to school"

This is what I announce,
sitting in the dingy living room
with a used couch we've covered
in Egyptian cotton sheets.

Only Spirit Week is left,
and I have none of that.

Sports Day.
Pajama Day.
Wacky Hair Day.
Mismatch Day.
Family Bankruptcy + Jail Day.

Can't face tomorrow.
The humiliation. The scandal.
What everyone will think of me.

"No, no. You just have to finish.
You don't have to be scared,"
Mom says as she surveys the apartment,
the paint peeling, the door frames loose.
"Hold your head up!"

I look at her. "We *just* ran away
from everything we've ever known.
We are here. In . . . basically in hell.
And you want *me* to just face it?
Are you out of your mind?"

Go On—Face It

Inside, though, I know
I need to. Look my life
dead in the eyes. Stare
into the unknown.

"I'm going outside,"
I announce. To no one,
apparently, since Mom has exited
this conversation and the room,
too caught up in her own drama.

The door slams too fast
and suddenly I'm face-to-face
with the same eager hand-raiser
I saw when we pulled in.

"Oh, hey," he says.
I look up into his eyes.
I do not need this.
Not for a second.

"Hi. I was just . . ."
I look around.
There is nothing
I was about to do.

"Name's Clint.
I was actually
about to knock.
Y'all need anything?
Or help with anything?"

"We're all good"

I lie. "Just . . . we're not even . . .
We're just here a couple weeks.
You don't have to worry.
I was just 'bout to take a walk."

He nods. "That's cool.
I don't wanna stand in your way,"
he says, clearly standing directly
in my way.

I don't even know where to walk
or go. So I just hold my hands up
and wind my way around him.
Look back, he's still there.

"It's Spirit Week at school,"
I say, and have no idea
why I am sharing that.
"I was just trying to get
some fresh air, or my energy up,
something like that. I don't know."

I look up to the sky,
eyes fill with tears.
If he can see it,
he doesn't let on.

Just asks if I want to see
how far the land goes.
I nod yes because I don't want
him to hear my voice crack.

So we walk. Far apart,
not even saying one word.

As if he knows not to ask
another question. Nothing
left for me to say. We look up,
the sky starting to be filled with stars.

He Speaks

His voice thick with a country accent.
"Last week of school for me too.
Spirit Week's a joke, right? No one wants
to dress alike or wear mismatched socks
or a jersey for some stupid sports team."

I look at him. "You serious?
You're not a Kentucky basketball fan?
I've never met a guy that's not obsessed."

"Well then, you've never met me.
Also . . . what's basketball again?
The one where they kick the ball, or . . . ?"

I laugh. The first time in days. He's serious.
At least I think he is?

"No, no, it's the hoop, right? Definitely the hoop.
And the points and the teams. Yeah, that's it.
Anyway, Spirit Week sucks. But at least summer's here.
You never know what can happen
with all those free weeks."

I nod this time. Smell the thick air
and let a few tears fall loose down my face.
What does it even matter anymore?
What do I have left to prove?

Sable Country Day

On my way to school,
I think about what I am used to.
The place I've spent the last
thirteen years of my life.
Most beautiful campus
in all of Kentucky, everything
blooming. Pristine. Perfection.
Parking lot full of high-end
luxury. Science lab. Swimming
pool. Tennis courts. Lounge.
Restaurant quality, locally
sourced food. Real chefs.
This is what the brochure
promised my family and me.
This has been my home
since I was four years old.
I cannot leave them hanging.
It is the one place that I can still
see myself. Can see my friends.
Can see all of us there together.
Standing through it. Strong.
Can see my graduation.
Can see closing out the year,
can see facing it. As one.
Trust that my friends
will have my back
once I let them in.

In the Parking Lot

Declan is waiting for me,
leaning on his Mercedes
scrolling through his phone.
Checking. Checking.
Watching for my car.
After a midnight text
he knows I am on the way.

"Chloe, hey?" He throws
both of his arms in the air
as if asking the ultimate
question. "Are you okay?
What is going on?" he asks,
holding his phone up to me
with my family photo
taking up the screen.
Bankrupt. Jail Time.
No Bail. Filling
every inch of his phone.
As if I don't already know.

"Well, look who's here?"

"Chloe Brooks, live and in person,"
Lily says, her voice coming in
like surround sound. She tilts
her head, looks straight at me.
"Can't believe you had the nerve
to show up back here."

"I want to talk . . . to both of you,"
I start, realizing I'm not sure
what it is I am supposed to say.

"What could you possibly
have to say to us?" Lily asks.
"Declan, I told you. The news
is all true. And they tried to take
all the rest of us down too."

They both stare at me
as a crowd starts to build
around us. A bunch of kids
holding their phones up
to hold on to this memory
of my takedown.

"Her family is broke.
And her dad is in jail
and likely going straight
to prison. Life as they know it
is over. And it almost ended
for us too, you know. The police

weren't only at your door,
they were at ours too.
You had to know about this!"

A few of the kids start to laugh,
think my life is a big joke.

"How broke are they?"

some ignorant freshman calls out,
as if he's in on the rant,
as if he knows anything
about me and my family.

"We're not! Look, my family
is just going through some stuff.
It's not . . . it's not the end of the world.
It's just some family business,"
I say, trying to get a hold of the situation,
realizing there's nothing to hang on to.

"Yeah, some *broke* family business,"
Lily says and smiles in my direction.
"I am so sorry for your loss," she continues,
as if she's at my funeral, and the truth is,
it feels like she is. Might as well bury me now.
My life—or the one I used to know—is over.
"Actually, I believe the exact word is *bankrupt*.
Like, they are totally and completely broke,
and your family almost took mine down with it.
If my mom and dad hadn't been smart enough
to not completely invest in all of your dad's businesses
and bizarre ideas, then we would've been broke too.
But now—thank god—it's just you and your family.
I really and truly can't believe you showed up
at Sable this morning," she says,
getting closer to me now.

"Fight, fight, fight!"

someone calls out, their phone on us,
in our faces. Declan is standing
to the side now, as if he's never even met me,
as if he didn't try to sleep with me,
claim some part of me, just days ago.
As if I have all but disappeared to him.

"Come on, I'm not gonna fight her.
It's not worth my time.
Not worth yours either,"
Lily says to Declan, pulling
him toward her.
"Don't worry,"
she calls out to everyone.
"She'll be paying for this . . . forever,"
and then she smiles at me again.
The kind that reminds me
that I own that smile, have given out
that smile too many times to count.
To people who I thought
I was better than, to underclassmen,
to new kids, to anyone who didn't
have as much as us. And we had
as much as you can imagine.
I know that smile,
perfected it
it was all mine.

Stay Silent

I don't respond, just shake
my head like I'm trying
to get lost inside of it.
Work to catch my breath,
or what's left of it.
Try to steady
my breathing down.
Head to my own SUV,
the one gifted for my sweet sixteen,
the only one we own now,
the one Mom and I suddenly share.
The two of us together in this loss.
Hide my tears.
Know that once I leave
I will never return,
except when I go online
and see my life
spliced together
with music and laughter,
with dance moves
and headlines
from the *Lexington Herald*.

"The Great Fall"
"One Family's Devastating Loss"
"The Once Wealthy Brooks Family"
"The Now Broke Brooks Family"
"What Will Happen Now?"

Chloe Brooks Was Here

She existed and now is gone.
She is survived by her mother
whose greatest achievement
was interior design and parties
with passed cocktails and tall,
tall flutes of champagne all night.
And her father who was the epitome
of wealth and excess. Owned a plane
and so many cars he had an extra
garage built beside the house.
She wanted to make her own way,
write her own future. The music
of her life. Songs telling stories
about who she was, who she
wanted so deeply to be.
It's true she was spoiled,
the most spoiled girl
in the whole wide world.
She had it all and now it is gone.
The girl who had it all
and lost it. Same sad, sad story
that she will keep on telling.
As long as anyone will listen.
This is it. Her story to tell.

WHAT IS LEFT TO TELL

It's All True

I spend the rest of the day chasing away
tears and longing for the past
out the car window. Studying
the hills of Kentucky as they rise up and fall.
Try to steady my heartbeat.
It's moving too fast.
I'm letting it go too far.
Want to hold it close to me,
not let anyone know the whole truth.
That we will have to completely vacate the house.
"Vacate." The word the lawyers used
on the phone this morning
when they asked about our possessions.
"Possessions." The word my mother uses
when she talks about everything she owns.
All of it.
I can see Declan laid out beside our pool
last summer, and Lily too—the way everyone
spent the afternoons lounging,
from the pool house to the diving board,
all of us sprawled around outside.
Just coasting. Just floating through the summer,
and now we're here—face-to-face,
with so much loss I can't catch my breath.
There it is again, and now it's gone.
Breathless. Lost.

Life Is OVER

This one at least.
The one I thought
would last forever.

One I've been holding,
clinging, dragging with me
is a thing of the past.

This is what it looks like
to have your whole life
unravel in front of
everyone you know.

I'm never going back.

I pull up to Limestone
and do everything possible
to avoid this group of kids
who seem to have nothing
better to do than sit around
at the picnic tables and hang out.

I do not wave.
I do not say hello.
I do not raise a hand
in their direction.
I do not holler my names
or answer when they call me.
I do not need a whole bunch
of new friends to treat me the way
my old friends just did.

This summer, I will cocoon.
Think I can still salvage
at least one of my camps
or a week in Europe.
Not gonna let this break me
or my spirit.

Let me introduce you
to the new and improved
Chloe Brooks.

Mom Is Sobbing

This is what I find
when I walk inside.
Huddled on the ground.
Heaving. I want to join her,
so I do. Both of us holding
on to each other so tight.

"How did I miss the signs?"
she asks, looking right at me.
Surveying the apartment,
and still looking for all
that we have lost.

"I know. I am so sorry, Mom.
But Dad will fix this. I know
he will."

She gives me a long look,
like she knows something
I do not. But I don't push
because I don't want to know.

"I don't want to leave you like this,"
I say and at this, she pulls back.

"Well, where in the world
would you be going?"

"Well, music camp, at least," I say,
trying to hold on to a summer
learning music production.
"I mean . . . haven't we already paid for that?"

You Cannot Be Serious

"Chloe Brooks, what in the world?
What money do you plan on using
when you get there?" Mom asks
and looks at me hard now.
"I am so sorry, but I think I raised you
to have no idea what money means.
Not even in the least little bit.
You have been along for the ride
with me and your father
and we haven't shown you nearly enough,
haven't shown you what really matters.
So what I can do for you this summer
is try and show you that money's not everything."

"Mom, come on. Are you for real?"
This is definitely not how I was raised.
She is absolutely right about that.

"Yes, this is the truth. We have to face it
and that's exactly what we're going to do."

And at this, I am scared. For everything.
But mostly the next two months.

I wake up covered in sweat

and completely freaking out.
I should be getting used to this.
I am jolted up by a voice
on the other side of the door.

"Anyone home?"
Both of us having fallen asleep
trying to forget the day
and the past altogether.

"There's some type of delivery
or something out here.
It's got your name on it.
Brooks, right?" the voice calls.

We look at each other,
trying to figure out who
ordered what. Mania.
That's what they call it
when people start to unravel
and lose control.
I look at Mom
who looks guilty.

"What? I got a few things.
Just essentials for us.
Before the cards were . . . I mean
we have to live, don't we?"

I look around the room. I nod.
This is a whole new way to live.

"Could somebody open the door?
'Cause there are a lot of boxes out here."

I look at Mom again.

"Don't be mad," she whispers.
"Could you go get it sorted?"

I shake my head, try and comb
through my hair and look at my mom.
How am I suddenly the adult here?

Clint Jackson

"At your service," he says
after saying his name all cocky
and bravado like. I do not like him.
Not even a little bit. Too country,
too know-it-all, too raises his ridiculous hand
even though he doesn't have a question.
Did I mention know-it-all? Or overconfident?
There is that too. In the way he leans upright
in our doorway. Behind him, stacks of boxes
that my mother has called to her. Her birthright.
Who does she think she is, trying to show me.
She is accustomed to being surrounded by excess.
Can't get enough. That's who I've always known her as.
So now I have to be here, face-to-face with him.
Clint Jackson. His name sounds like a country song
that I do not want to know the lyrics to. He studies
me, our apartment, the sky, the dirt and grass
he's standing on. Tilts his head in that same way,
as if he knows more than we do or appears to.
As if there are a whole bunch of words he's aching
to say and a whole trash load of opinions he is
bursting at the seams to get off his chest.

I Don't Like It

Him or the way he stands,
or this complex or this neighborhood
or the way my mom is acting out,
and I especially don't like myself.
Yes, I am sick to death of my own
thoughts and fears. Hate the way
I have shown up, hate the me
I have gotten used to and the one
I am having to say goodbye to.
Yes, that is who I don't like the most.

Me.

"We do not need your help"

I say. Clear and to the point.

He looks at me for a beat. Stares.
Does not try and look in our apartment,
but if he did, all he would see
would be empty. A bunch of nothing.
Save for a small couch
and two single beds
in two tiny rooms.

"You sure? Because there's a lot
of boxes out here. Like *a lot*.
And I'm happy to carry them inside."

"You don't work for us you know?"

He stops a second longer. Puts both arms
up in the air. Not like he's giving up,
but like he has more questions.
Like he's trying to figure out
who we are and why or if he cares.

"No, I know that. I didn't say I did.
This is just me helping out. It's just me
being a neighbor who sometimes
carries boxes for people who need help,
and it just seemed like y'all needed
a couple extra hands. That's all I'm saying."

"Well, this is our family business.
It is private and we don't really need

extra hands or extra help. We're not elderly
or in serious need of anything.
We are perfectly capable of taking good,
good care of ourselves, so you can just
see your way home." I smile
a sick one, the same one Lily gave me
that makes me feel embarrassed
and furious at the same time.

He stands in the doorway

his arms resting at his sides,
head tilted up toward the sky.

I do not close the door
but do not invite him inside.

He is studying and analyzing me
and I am completely over it.

But I guess I'm doing the same,
trying to figure out what's next.

Game time. Where I pretend
this is not where we live.

Where I imagine a future
that isn't the one I'm in.

Where I keep it all closed in.
Our story, the lies, our history.

He doesn't need to know
any more than he already does.

Nosy, I think. Looking back at him
like we're in some of old-school

staring contest. Who will look away
first? Who will break eye contact?

Not me, I think. Arms crossed.
My eyes daring him to say more.

"Are you for real right now?"

he asks, starting to laugh a little.
"Seriously, I can't tell if you're joking
or if you're serious. Uhh . . . I was just . . .
I was just trying to say hi and check
in with y'all. We do this around here.
Maybe you're not used to . . . us or this,
or maybe . . . I don't know. This whole
place has each other's backs. That's it.
That's what we do, who we are.
All of us grew up here so we know
what everyone needs and we help
whenever we can. That's just us."

"I didn't even ask"

I say, knowing it's the wrong thing
when I see his face. I do not know
how to tell him I feel ashamed
about myself and my family.
Don't know how to admit
our mistakes or that me and Mom
seem like the only ones
still out in the world
paying for it.
I can't find the words
to say my friends are out there
talking all the trash and spreading
all the rumors, upping all the lies.
I don't dare say this place
makes me feel sad and depressed
with its run-down everything
and that my family
is the reason why.
So I act out. Something
I am used to doing
when I don't get what I want.
"Spoiled" would be one of the words.
"Entitled" is the other.
Can't help it. Don't care anymore
what Clint Jackson thinks about me
or us. Just want him out of my doorway
and especially my life.

"Look"

he says, "I don't wanna cause any problems.
You don't have to like me or be friends
with me or anything like that. I just
wanted to show up if you needed me is all."

"We won't even be here long enough
for me to not like you, okay?
We are just here for like a second,
a couple of weeks at the most, so, uh . . .
we don't have to be friends or get to know
each other. Not even a little bit."

"Oh, wow. Okay, I hear you. I got it.
Don't worry," he says back, slow and cool.
Not matching my anger or my loud
and in your face one bit. Not getting bigger
when I get bigger or angrier or rowdier.
Just chill, just laid-back. He smiles, even,
and that makes me burn even more.

"What does that mean?
What are you smiling about?"

"Nothing, I just . . . I like all this energy here.
It was getting kinda quiet around these parts.
You're bringing something
a little . . . unexpected. A little wild.
I can get with that."

"Get with what? You are not getting with *this*,"
I say. He looks back, shocked.

"That is definitely not what I meant.
No, no. I just . . . I meant . . . I was just saying
I liked being caught off guard . . . Not that I . . .
uhh . . . Never mind. I just . . . You want help
with the boxes or what?"

I look at him one last time
and the piles of junk my mom has ordered,
clearly not understanding what *spend no money*
actually means.

"Umm . . . yeah. Yes, we could use some help,"
I admit and open the door just a little.

All of a Sudden

My life is unraveling.
Coming apart at the seams.
A thread that gets pulled
and then keeps running
and running along
with no end in sight.
Just unspooling
right before my eyes.

One week ago, my family
was one of the wealthiest
ones in the Bluegrass
if not the country.

Today, we are left
with nothing. One
rogue credit card
that won't last
and one apartment complex
that is crumbling around us.
Just enough to keep
us afloat. Along
with everyone here.

It's true, money
gave me the feeling
of being the only one,
most special, the prize,
the make it to the top
girl. Whatever you want
girl. So when I look

in the mirror and do not
see that same girl,
I do not know
what to think,
how to act,
who to be,
what I need,
what's next,
how to stay
moving
at all.

And I Miss Everything

The way I never had to ask
for anything I wanted.
It just arrived. I dreamed it
and it was there. I miss
my horses. All of them.
Boarded now
and being ridden by girls
who are not me. At stables
that are not ours. I miss
the wind washing over me
and the speed over the hills.
I miss our porch and pool,
my friends hanging out
with no worry about time
or obligations. Declan, Lily,
all the kids who'd hang
forever at our place. Miss
making out in the back seat
and missing curfew because
no one was ever waiting up,
because my mom and dad
had their own lives without
me. Had their businesses
and were always so busy
they didn't notice my wild
or out of control. I miss
being out of control. Now
there is a quiet I am not at all
used to. Silence. So I am left
alone with my thoughts
and that feels terrifying.

Text Lily

You there?
Can we talk?
We're better than this.
You have to know
I didn't know.
And sorry we got your family
all wrapped up in this mess.
And I miss you.
Call me?

Lily almost texts

...

Then silence.
Nothing at all.

Text Declan

...

Pause.
Then stop.
What would I even say?
Who would I try to pretend
that I am?

Summer for Real

Each day, I wake
stuck to my sheets.
Skip the last days.
School as I know it
seems to be over.
Wonder about air
and what will keep
me cool. Nothing
at this point. Heat
trapped inside. All
of me restless. Mom
in the kitchen ranting
about Dad and her life
coming apart alongside
mine. Windows open,
no breeze, just stale,
just stuck, just aching
for something to do
or someone to call.
Boredom snakes around
me. My phone a time
bomb. No calls or texts.
My whole family
having been shunned,
taken out of rotation.
Now that we have
nothing, no calls
come in for donations
or benefits to celebrate
our success and money.
No money means

no urgency
or frantic messages
or buildings with our name
or galas or invitations.
Outcast. On the outside.
And stuck inside
a crumbling complex
that we are still
responsible for.

"Laundry!"

Mom announces, as if we're winning
some lottery or prize. "We need clothes,"
she says, eyeing me. I'm sprawled out
on the couch, wearing the same things
I wore yesterday and the day before.
Who is even seeing me anymore?
My whole amazing wardrobe is wasting away.

"Oh yeah, please! Can you wash sheets too?
It's so hot without air conditioning.
I'm always sweating through everything,"
I say, try and cut the TV on and remember
we have no cable, no internet.

"Um . . . yes, please wash the sheets, clothes,
and especially the towels," my mom says,
standing in front of me with pillowcases
full of our dirty laundry. *What in the world?*

"Me?" I ask, staring dead at my mom
who clearly has no idea who she's talking to.
"I can't do . . . I don't know . . . What? How?
Why? I . . . You know I can't do that . . . I don't . . ."

"Chloe, you can do this. It is just laundry.
It is just washing our clothes, which need it.
Badly! And I have to visit the lawyer today,
so you have to start pitching in around here."

I look at my mom, whose gray hair is just
starting to grow in. Both of us look ragged,
rough around the edges.

"Fine. I'll do it. But where's the washing machine?"
I ask, walking down the small hallway.
"I didn't see it when we moved in."

"We don't have one, Chloe," she says, saying
my name like she's exasperated, worn out.
"It's in the middle of the complex."

"What?! You mean I have to wash our underwear
with everyone else's underwear? Soooo gross."

My mom nods. I am dying inside.

Clean Clothes

The building that houses the washing machines
and all the dryers is dead in the middle of the yard.
There are vending machines full of chips and sodas,
and help wanted signs, and flyers for events, gatherings.

As soon as I walk in, I see an older woman
and a younger woman,
one loading a dryer and the other folding clothes.
They wave in my direction. Why is everyone so friendly
here? Like everyone is in on all your business.

"Hi, I'm Natalia," the younger woman says. She looks
about my age with her hair in a long braid down her back.

"Chloe," I say. "Nice to meet you both," I add,
remembering my manners, realize I need to pull it together.

The older woman nods, continues folding.
"This is my abuela. She pretends she doesn't speak English,
but she's lying. She one hundred percent
understands everything.
Don't you, Abuela?" Natalia smiles at me
and gives her abuela a hug. "Me, I speak Spanish, English,
and Country. You could say I am multilingual.
My family's from Mexico, but I grew up right here.
Bluegrass-born. Kentucky all the way. You?"

"Yeah . . . I'm from Kentucky too. Right here . . . Well . . .
just outside of downtown. We just moved . . . We're, uh . . .
going through some renovations, so we're here for now,"
I add, realize I don't even know enough to build

a good lie or a good fake life. I look away, pull clothes
out of our pillowcases and start to stuff all of them,
every last article, into the biggest washing machine.
Natalia and her abuela both stare at me. Watching.
Judging maybe? I can't tell. I push it all deep down
and go for my detergent, have no idea what I'm doing.
"Did you need something?" I ask.

"No, it's just . . . you might want to separate the colors,
because it could bleed together and might ruin your . . ."

"I think I know how to do this, okay. I don't need
any help. Thank you anyway," I add, sickly sweet.

Mess

Even the laundry room is a dump in this place.
Everything falling in on itself. The machines
are all dirty, the space not cared for or cared
about. All of it rusting or peeling or cracking.

This is not the kind of space I am used to,
not the kind of work I have ever done, or even
been asked to do. I do not need advice or ideas
on how to manage my life by people I don't know.

So I keep on doing things my own way, ignore
Natalia and her abuela giving me looks of pity
or at least that's what it feels like. Try to hide
my own disgust at this work, this place, my life.

"I can't live like this"

I say to no one in particular,
even though Mom is staring down
at the wreck of our clothes,
all of them bleeding together.
I have ruined a whole load of laundry.
All of it turning deep red and purple.
A mess, mimicking our whole lives.

"They offered to help you?
And you said no?
Why did you say no to help?"
she asks, holding up her once
white shirt. "What were you thinking?"

"Well, you didn't feel the need to help me.
And I figured I could do it on my own."

"You cannot. Clearly you cannot."

"Well, maybe that's because you and Dad
never ever taught me how to do anything.
At all. I don't know how to do stupid laundry
or stupid cooking, or cleaning. I don't *do*
any of that, or at least I never did before,
so how can you expect me to now?"

"Chloe, we can't do *nothing* anymore.
That's not an option this summer.
We actually have to survive and take care
of ourselves, okay? This is not a joke.
This is not summer camp."

"It's definitely not summer camp, Mom.
At every summer camp I have ever been to
THEY DO YOUR LAUNDRY FOR YOU!"

"This whole place can suck it!"

"It's true," I say, louder now,
pacing the living room
that is the size of my old closet.
"All I can see are dusty roads
and this crappy, ugly carpet
in this crappy, ugly apartment building.
Like it's a place I just landed.
Like I'm some alien body sent down to try
and figure out what the hell to do with all
of this empty time in my life.
And I now realize that I have zero life skills
in the actual godforsaken world."

"Chloe, come on. Buck up," Mom tries
to stop my monologue, but I am just
getting started and I want her to hear
everything that's running around
in my mind.

"Buck up? Forget that. I am alone and scrambling.
And this stupid apartment is too small
to hold me and all my ideas about trying to get out.
I am embarrassed to tell my friends
who have all dropped off the face of the planet.
Here I am. Dead to the world. Look at me.
Lost in the sea of disgusting bugs and roaches
on basically a big ole farm outside of the city.
This is the story, except it's not that funny to me.
It's scary and sad and all completely true.
This shithole can suck it," I shout.

"Just suck it up"

I hear called back to me. And suddenly
I remember that all the windows are wide open,
even if the blinds are pulled down.

I jump off the bed, pull open the blinds,
and yell back, "What did you say?"
Freaked out now that someone
has been listening to me,
that some creeper is just sitting
at my window and listening for me,
paying the closest of attention to me.
"Who is that anyway?"

"Your neighbors." I hear the voice again.
I turn my light off and look outside.
I see four people lit only by a candle
sitting at one of the run-down picnic tables
in the circle. Some of the same ones
I saw last week hanging out together.

"Clint," I hear the one sitting close by say.
Of course, it is the famous Clint Jackson.
The one and only. *Punk*, I think.
"This is James and Skye and Natalia.
We, uh . . . live in this *shithole* you now call home."

"I wasn't even talking to you"

I say. Flustered. Embarrassed
that they heard me, that I cannot
figure out how to keep my mouth shut.

"We know that," Skye says.
"And believe me, we didn't wanna hear
anything you had to say just now.
But listen, princess, it kinda sounds like
you're not really in your castle anymore."

"What did you say?" I ask,
leaning out the window now.
I can smell the air thick with summer,
sweat starting at my temples.
"I never said I was a princess!"

"Well, anyone who gets their laundry
done at some fancy summer camp
prolly has some princess tendencies,
am I right?" she asks, and they all laugh.
I can hear it ricochet off the night sky.
"And besides that, I think all the bugs
and roaches and rodents are truly
offended by your attitude.
You're gonna need to pull it together
if you're gonna live here. And, honey,
you *do* live here. With them. And us."

The End of the World

"Don't remind me!" I shout
and slam my window shut.
It's so rickety in the frame
it almost shatters.
This is the definition of shithole.
Don't they know that?
Who do they think they are?
Treating me like some entitled jerk,
which I am not. I am just
working things out and trying
desperately to figure out
just where I landed.
And now these punks
are getting all up
in every piece of my life,
acting like they know me
or anything about me.
I do not belong here
or anywhere close to here.
This is not my home.

All of Me Is Fired Up

Mad as hell, I start to pace the room,
talking myself down. *What in the world?*
Where am I? And how did I get here?

There is a knock at the door.
I look outside.
It's Clint.
So slim you can hardly see him
if he turns to the side. Tall and gangly.
Jerk, I think again. He's got cutoff shorts on
and an old baggy T-shirt. Baseball cap
and a pair of thick black glasses.
Some of him looks like he fits
and some of him looks like
he could come back with me
to my side of town.

"What do you want?" I ask,
leaning on the door

'Seriously? Let's call a truce.
Just come on out here.
Might as well meet the people you live with,"
he says and then smiles right at the peephole
and his teeth are as straight and white
as I've ever seen. Horse teeth
is what my mom used to call them,
and dammit—they're pretty.
I open the door despite myself
and walk outside.

Night Sky

The yard is full of fireflies
bumping on and off. Thick
country air surrounds us.
Feel like I've been sweating
all week. Clint, James, Skye,
Natalia. I say their names
in my head, try to remember
who these new people are.
I am not a child after all.
Though maybe I have been
acting like one the past week.
They are leaned out over
the picnic table. Sprawled
and look so relaxed.
Nothing to do on a Friday
night except hang and let
the night happen.
Every Friday for me
used to be parties, events,
shopping, traveling. A whole
calendar of ways to disappear
or ways to forget problems.
Things to do. I always
used to have things to do.
Skye is telling a story,
her laugh echoing
through the night.
Natalia and James
laughing loud with her.
It's clear they know
each other so well

that this night is easy
and natural and so
laid-back I don't know
how I'll fit in.
I sit just the same.

Study them

their styles mostly and the way they look
so casual and put together with such ease.
Skye stands out the most with her short locs
and steady stare. Her and James must be twins,
the way they mirror each other. Dark brown skin
and easy smiles. It's clear she's got everyone's
attention. Long legs tucked up underneath
of her, cutoff shorts and a T-shirt that hangs
off her shoulders. Fact is, they're all wearing
some version of this. Only difference
is that James's hair is cut close and Clint's
got a mess sprouting out. Natalia has hers up now
in a messy bun. No pretense. No extra.
No having to look a certain way or play a specific part.
Her skin is lighter brown and Clint looks like
he's already been out in the sun all month long.
A steady tan and slight sunburn across his nose
beneath those glasses. I cannot put my finger
on who these kids are.

And can't tell if I need to get to know them
or not. Unsure how long my life will be
steady here or if we're just dipping in. This
and my whole life feels uncertain.
They somehow welcome me anyway. No real
concern for my outburst or my stuck-up ways.
All open arms here. And I realize—I am thankful.

How do they all look so comfortable, so all in?
I try not to study my own self too much,
stuck in one of my fitted sundresses. Overdressed
and somehow feel more out of place than ever.

"Sorry you heard me"

"I didn't know the window was open,"
I start, realizing I should be the one
apologizing.

"That's what you're sorry for?" Natalia asks.

"Not for calling this place . . . what was it . . .
crappy and ugly and small?" Skye adds.

They look right at me. This is not funny,
but I feel like the joke.

"No, no. I meant . . . I didn't mean
for you to hear me. I didn't want . . ."

"No, that sounds right," James says.
They study me right back.
"I wouldn't have wanted anyone to hear me
talk about somebody's home in that way either.
Look, we all know this is not the nicest
place to live. Fact is, it's a dump.
They used to take care of it back in the day,
but now we don't even see the super
and it takes weeks to fix anything around here.
It's basically falling apart, so we get that.
We're not proud of the place either,
but it's not our fault. It's whoever owns this trash heap."

I nod. See my family and know we
are definitely the ones to blame.

"But it's full of good people and my best friends," he continues, looking around the table.

Who We Are

"You might wanna take some time
to get to know us. Who we are,
what we're about. Before judging
or getting any wrong ideas," Skye says,
seeming to soften up a bit.
"Because you seem to have a lot
of opinions about this place and us.
Seem to think you got it all figured out.
Maybe it's not us you need to accept.
Maybe it's you?"

I lose my breath for a second,
feel like I might faint in the heat,
in the moment, in what feels like
exposure, acknowledgment,
vulnerability, and I almost
can't take this fact.

"I'm sorry"

I say. And mean it this time,
especially when I think about
who is responsible,
who should be taking care
and tending to Limestone.

I do not say that my old home
was big and beautiful,
but dishonest and cold
and corrupt.

These are truths I hold
deep inside of me.
Can't let them find out
who the real me is.

Clint Starts

"I'll go first. Introduce myself and all.
Clint Jackson. You already know that.
I was born and raised
right here in Lexington, Kentucky.
Home of the thoroughbreds.
Home of the bourbon.
Home of the Bluegrass.
You get the idea."

They all agree. It's clear they are used to
Clint saying a whole buncha words
a whole buncha ways.

"Live here with my uncle. Born into horse country
and been a hot-walker—helped calm the horses
down after they raced. Been riding all my life,
as long as I can remember at least,
and helped with cleaning and training.
Live over in apartment eight.
Been working my whole life it feels like,
so I can cook, I can clean,
I can definitely do laundry,"
he adds, winking in my direction.
They have clearly been talking about me.
"And been living here in Limestone
since I was born. This is home."

Natalia Says

"Yeah, welcome to Limestone. It's definitely
its own thing over here."

"What do you mean?" I ask. Wanting to know
what I'm missing, what I'm trying to figure out.

Natalia looks at me like she's tired already.
Maybe she is, since I didn't even pay attention
in the laundry room. I try to listen this time.

"What I mean is that this area is kinda known
for being everybody. There's no Black
or Brown or White section of town,
or only Spanish-speaking side,
it's just all of us together. Working class basically.
People who drive buses, janitors, maids,
nannies, gardeners, short-order cooks,
people who work at fast-food joints, long-haul
truck drivers, people who get paychecks in all
sorts of different ways. People paid in cash
or under the table. People who are here
without papers and who do all the jobs
that support the community. Undocumented
people and struggling ones and their families.
It's just a bunch of people trying to make it work."

I nod along, but do not say that it seems like
she's talking about all the people who have been working
to make my family and our lives look good and easy.

"Here, there's poor White folks living next to
poor Brown and Black folks too. In it together.
It's the way I've always known it to be. Same
in our school. Linked together. Known these kids
since I was born. We are legacy around here,"
Skye adds and flashes that same smile.

Suddenly, I want to know them more.
Clint and James too. Take notes.
Try and figure out my place in it all.

My Turn

"So what's your story?" Clint asks,
and I am at a loss for words.

What story do I tell them?

Do I tell the story of excess and more
or do I tell it straight up?

Do I say I was born into everything
and given anything I could ever want?

Do I say money was never anything
I ever worried about? Never anything
that stayed on my mind? Just happened
that we had it all, all the time.

Do I lie? Pretend I'm something
anything
that I'm not?

Can't get the words
to tumble out of my mouth,
so I say nothing.

What I Do Not Say

I do not tell them that this apartment complex
is owned by my family—that my parents
own, or used to own, dozens of complexes
all across the city. I do not say
that they owned three hotels and car washes
and truck washes from eastern to western Kentucky
and beyond. I do not say that their name is on buildings
at the University of Kentucky
and the University of Louisville
and Eastern and Western,
Transylvania and Bellarmine,
and on and on. I do not tell them
that my parents are some of the biggest donors
to Keeneland and Churchill Downs
and the Kentucky Center for the Performing Arts,
and that I am pretty sure that the only reason
I have stayed at the top of my classes at Sable
is because my parents have gifted the school
with an auditorium and a science lab.
My parents are accustomed to getting everything
they want and can pay for. I leave that out of my life story.

"Yeah, I was born here too," I say.

At least that is the truth.

The Singing Starts

As if I am not even here anymore,
Skye and James pull out a notebook
with what looks like lyrics,
and so does Clint, a tiny one
from his back pocket that I notice
he carries everywhere with him.
A guitar appears beside Natalia.
Clint starts a beat on the picnic table
and they begin to harmonize.
And my heart and breath get caught
right in the middle of my chest.

They sound unlike anything
I have ever heard. A little pop,
a little bluesy, but mostly country,
or at least that's what I think,
but I'm trying to not even think
at all anymore, and so I close my eyes
and listen for the words, the poetry,
the sound of Skye and James together,
the lilt, the lushness of the sound.

Want to remember the days.
Let me always stay. Play.

Will you play me a song
that takes all night long?

Let it last, linger, still me.
Let it burn, singe, play me.

Let it twirl, dance, rhyme me.
Let it jump, turn, time me.

Let this feeling last, last, last.

Wild Clapping

I can't even help myself
because at the end,
I am on my feet
clapping and smiling.
Unexpected,
embarrassed,
but shocked
at the sound,
at the night,
at their voices,
and the way
they sound
so
damn
free.

Shook

"What was that?" I ask.
Want to know more,
suddenly as much as possible.
"Who are you all?"

"James, Skye, Clint, Natalia,"
James says, laughing. "Remember?
We just told you. That's who we are."

"No, no, I mean. Are you a group?
Like a band? Or a . . . Do you record?
Are you on a label?"

"Yeah, we're actually touring
all summer long. Down South,
out West. Course Europe in July."

I stop. They sound both brilliant
and unexpected. And they are taking
my entire summer away from me.
I stare at them. They are silent
looking back at me, then each other.
Then they all bust out laughing
and I realize. I am the joke.

"Ha ha! So funny," I say,
embarrassed again. "I just . . .
I just meant you all are . . .
awesome. I mean, you could
be touring all those places for real."

"You wanna be our manager?"
James asks. I smile back.

Do not tell them that I might as well.
That they sound like this Kentucky night,
all full and warm and perfect.
Do not tell them I wanna join them too,
been writing songs since middle school.
That I have nothing better to do
and it might just give me something
to look forward to.

Good Night

Clint walks me to my apartment door.
I do not ask him to and almost tell him
that I know the way. But part of me
wants to know more.

"You liked that, huh?" he asks,
doing that lean thing
where his body is half on the wall
and half gliding into what feels like thin air.

"Seriously, you all sound soooo,
soooo good. It was . . . wild.
And what was that sound?
I couldn't place it, but somehow
it sounded like . . . home. Like here."

He nods. "Yeah. Thanks.
It's got a little R & B, little country,
little banda, little Tejano, little banjo,
picnic table drums, got our own songs.
We're kinda trying to be our own thing
but definitely have the people we love.
You know, Carolina Chocolate Drops
mixed with a little Selena, Jason Isbell,
and some Dolly Parton, Aaron Neville,
Yola, Maren Morris . . . you get the idea."

I absolutely do not get the idea.
It sounds all over the place
and I don't even know half
the people he just mentioned.

"Right," I say instead. Nodding.

"If you wanted, I could make you
a playlist? I mean . . . if you were interested."

"Yeah, no. Please. Yeah. I'm, uhhh . . .
I'm definitely interested."

We exchange phones, put our numbers in.

He writes "Clint Jackson" as the first name
and "AT YOUR SERVICE" as the last.

Welcome to Limestone Playlist

Clint sends me all the people to check out,
says this is just the beginning and everyone
has to start somewhere.

Texts:
Love these. Check out.
Find what you love too.

Carolina Chocolate Drops
Jason Isbell
Dolly Parton
Aaron Neville
Lil Nas X
Darius Rucker
Valerie June
Yola
Maren Morris
Linda Martell
Ingrid Contreras
Amythyst Kiah
Helen Ochoa
Tina Turner
Selena
Zoe Speaks

A Week Later

Mom is in the kitchen cooking.
In a heavy skillet, the corn bread
sizzling and spitting.
She is at the stove now,
a place she has not been
in so long that it stops me in the hallway.
I watch her. A bigger sprout of gray
popping up at the roots of her hair.
One arm hooked on her hip.
The small radio playing Trisha Yearwood
and her shoulders going up and down.
This is the same mom who hosted
the Derby gala last year for two hundred people,
all drunk and swaying to the jazz ensemble.
The same mom who has hosted dozens
of garden parties with bouquets
that littered the foyer and the staircase.
Same mom who hired decorators and bartenders
and caterers and drivers
and nannies and gardeners
and people to clean and maintain
and dust and most especially cook.
I have never, not once in my whole life,
seen my mom at the kitchen stove
and so this is new.
Something to witness for sure.

"You're cooking?" I ask—shocked and concerned.
Will it even be edible?

I stand far enough away and just stare
in disbelief,
in embarrassment,
in question,
in awe,
in all the emotions that keep on getting kicked up
every second that we live this new life.
I want to go home is what I think.
But stay perfectly still. Watching.

"Yes. And stop staring. It's rude," she says.
"Grab a plate. It's almost done anyway."

She starts to sing

her voice high and loud.
Singing in that same free way
that I heard the other night.
No pretense, no extra, no over-the-top.
The windows are all thrown open.
I look outside the window and Clint is sitting
with Skye and James on one of the picnic tables
in the middle of the courtyard. Clearly
this is their meeting spot. Can't get away from it.
Clint raises his arm up in a wave when he sees me.
I duck down and cover my face.

What is this feeling? And why is it happening to me?

"What is wrong with you?" Mom asks
and squats down beside me.

"Nothing. Get up," I whisper.

"What are we doing down here on the floor?"
Mom asks.
She is covered in grease from the bacon
from the morning, from the unease
of all this newness. Of all this
unbalance. This new act
we're playing at.

"Mom, could you please get up?
This is embarrassing," I say.
She looks at me and starts to laugh
right in my face.

"Is it a boy? The same one we met last week?"
She rises up to look,
then waves out the window
and I want to die for sure now.

Mom Sabotages My Life

"Y'all hungry?" she yells.
And they must be nodding and saying yes
because the next thing I know,
they are walking in the screen door
and sitting at the card table
that we're using as a kitchen table
and I haven't even washed my face yet
or my hair. Or brushed my teeth.
But here they are, and they don't
even know me or trust me.
And maybe I don't trust myself either
but we're here. All of us. Mom pulls out
two more folding chairs and gets us plates
and then loads them up with grits, bacon,
and the best corn bread I've ever tasted. Hers.
Her mother's recipe or her granny's. I don't even know.
And realize there's so much of my life that's unknown.
So I go on and eat. Mom turns the radio up louder.
It's still the country station, but I don't even mind,
and Skye, James, and Clint know all the words,
so they sing along with my mom too. *Unbelievable.*
So I just keep my head down and make another plate.

Washing Dishes

I pour so much soap on the dishes,
Mom takes my hands and helps me.

"Here, let me show you." So she does.
After everyone has left and they've all
shared stories and exchanged recipes.
Mom's corn bread, fried chicken, dumplings,
none of which I have ever had.
She wrote them all down, handed out copies.

"Why didn't you ever make that for us?"

She pauses. Sits down, puts her head
in both of her hands. Pauses just before
the tears come rolling out.

"I don't want to say I came from nothing.
That sounds awful and sad. And in some ways
it is, it was. We did not have much. At all.
Grew up right here in Limestone. Daddy
taking care of everyone else's problems.
A super never sleeps. Mama cleaning up
over in all the big houses downtown.
She'd come home and her hands'd be raw.
Both of them tired. Exhausted. So I cooked.
Every night. My own grandparents
teaching me. Got us a little plot of land
for a garden. Fed the whole complex.
Felt like they taught me how to do everything.
And what did I teach you to do?
Call someone to help, right?"

She sighs heavy. And I realize what she is saying
is that I cannot do anything. And she is right.

"I forgot who I was"

"When I met your father, I became someone
to be seen. Something to be shown off.
Miss Kentucky, you know? That's all I was."

I did know this much. Mom as model,
as beauty pageant winner, best of the South,
cover of *Lex Country Magazine*. Known
to everyone by her long, loose, wavy hair
and perfect skin. Hourglass. All the things
that make a Southern woman proud.

"I loved him. I still do . . . of course.
I love him. I just became something else,
someone else entirely when I was with him.
And I'm having a hard time remembering
and still trying to love the person I used to be."

Tell Me the Truth

"Mom, why did you let your whole self
disappear? And why didn't you tell me
about your past, about who you were?
What made you think I didn't want to know?"

She leans forward, reaches out to hold my hands.
I move to put my arms around her and see
she needs me as much as I need her.
But I push on. Don't want her to get away
with it so easy. She's a part of it too.

"Our whole life is gone. All seventeen years
feels like it was just a fake. And you
went along with it. Didn't question it,
just let Dad do whatever he wanted
and for what?" I ask.

"To get out of this place," she says,
looking right into my eyes. "To leave."
Shame filling us both up. "Your dad fell hard
for me. Whether it was how I looked
or how I made him feel . . . it didn't matter.
I loved the way I felt when I was with him.
He promised a different life, a new way.
More than I ever had. Swore our life
would be easy. Would be better.
And he was right. So that's what we did.
And I know I'm a part of this. I know.
But what am I supposed to do about it?
I don't even know who I am anymore."

At Night

Alone in the bedroom, I can hear Mom
crying through the thin walls. Weeping.

Both of us trying to figure out who it is
we even are anymore? Searching, scrambling.

What am I supposed to tell her
when I have no idea either?

Lost and scared of what's next.
I stop, take a breath, pick up my phone.

I have no one to call or text. No one
who will reply. No friends. No other family.

Just Mom. Just me. Just counting the minutes
and seconds until someone sends help.

Dad has disappeared, but our life with him
feels like it was a big mirage, not real, not true.

Still afraid. Still trying to figure out who it is
we are supposed to be without all the stuff.

Without all the extra around us. Always.
The picture of perfection. The flawless.

We stay in our own rooms. Exposed. Lost.
Trying to find each other at the same time.

By the Next Weekend—I Rewind

I find Clint at the picnic tables.
"Let's start again," I say.
"Have a redo. From the beginning."
And what I mean is: *Pretend our last meetings*
did not happen. Go back in time and imagine
I am someone you have never met.
Forget about all my failings
and how I showed up the first time.
Forget we ever met in the first place. Please?

"A do-over, huh? Yeah,
maybe that'd be a good thing,"
Clint says and smiles with all his teeth.
Shrugs his shoulders
and does that lean back thing
that I am starting to get used to.
Maybe he will not fall after all.
Maybe he will hang right there
in the balance. Straddling the line
between right here and the past.
The way I am doing always.

"My name is Chloe Brooks.
I just moved into the building
across the way."
I point to our apartment and try to ignore
the peeling paint and the grass that's grown
tall and unruly all around us.

"I'm Clint. Clint Jackson.
Welcome to the Stables."

"The Stables?" I say, repeating him,
realizing I don't know a thing
about Clint or his friends at all.

"Yeah. That's what we call it anyway,
since this land sits on an old horse farm.
And neighbors on each side still keep 'em."

"Nice," I say.

"Not really," he says, looking around.
We both smile, but I feel gutted inside.

Family Legacy

I am at all times embarrassed that this
is what my family is leaving behind,
that this is what we
will become known for.
This is the history
they will tell about us:
of neglect
and abandonment.

He points far away,
past the edge of the complex,
and I can see open fields
lush with blooming foxglove,
marigolds popping yellow,
bergamot and bluets,
all deep purples and violets,
all names I know from studying
my own yard full of wildflowers
planted to look like they belong
in front of a house rather than
growing reckless in all that green.
The horses dot the distance
and the air is thick and humid
around us. Circling and holding
us in. We are just outside of city limits
so you can see the skyline of downtown
but you're still out a ways.
Both in it and away from it.

"You ride?" Clint asks

and I look back at the horses again.
Think about my own family farm.

"Yeah," I reply.
I don't tell him about our own stable.
All of the horses we owned,
the ones who've raced in Derby Days,
how we'd pride ourselves
on the animals and their upkeep.

I look around this property
and realize that maybe we took
better care of our animals
than we did the people
who live in our buildings.
Our properties.
Which are not ours anymore
anyway.

"Me too," Clint says
knocking me back into the moment,
into the now we are talking about.
"You wanna meet my horse?"

"Really? You have a horse?"

"Well, it's not really mine,
but that's what I call it. Come on.
I know the neighbors on both sides.
They let me ride long as I help.

Do a little cleanup of the stables,
a little hot-walking after the horses train.
A little of this and that," he explains.

"I'll show you."

Make Our Way

We start over to the stables together.
The grass is high against my ankles
and the sun is making the sky full
of deep oranges and reds—all yellow
and peeling open in the sky. Everything
feels alive and full of color.
I am dressed in fitted jeans and a silk top,
my hair blown and curled Kentucky-style.
Wedge sandals that I want to throw off
my feet and me. All of it feels out of place.
None of it matters to me anymore. All
of my clothes seem too complicated, too extra.
Clint has hay in his hair, baggy cargo shorts on,
and his gray socks pulled all the way up.
He's not the hot I am used to,
but somehow he is hot just the same.
And I am not totally used to feeling
this kind of heat.

My mind runs to Declan

and his all the time slick looks.
His hair gelled to perfection.
His endless weightlifting
and soccer goals. His world travels
and how he would talk and talk
about all the stamps in his passport.
I think about his French, and his kissing,
his Escalade, and the jewelry he'd give
to keep me excited and on edge.
Think about his all the time extra.
The way he treated me
like a trophy. The way my dad
treated my mom too. Display girl.
Perfect. Poised. In control.
Always to be looked at
and controlled and studied.
Kept in a box. Seen not heard.
Celebrated not valued.

I am not his anymore.
Throw off my sandals
and let my feet
and my body
and all of me
be
free.

"You lost?"

Clint asks. "What're you thinking about?"
We're almost at the stables and my mind
is wandering so much he notices.

"Oh, nothing, just my ex-boyfriend.
Or I guess he's my ex-boyfriend.
I don't really know. We just kind of . . .
stopped talking, stopped hanging out."

"You got ghosted?" he says, "Damn,
that's harsh. I'm sorry about that.
You go to school together?
What's his name? Maybe I know him."

"Oh, I don't think so, my school is
all the way outside of here. You don't . . .
His name is Declan," I admit.

"His name is Declan? That's not even . . .
that's not even a real name. That's like
something out of *Gossip Girl*
or some evil character
set out to destroy the earth.
That's not a . . . real name, you know?"

"Oh, look who is so open-minded
and kindhearted and neighborly now, huh?"

Clint smiles in my direction.

"Look, I'm just saying,
based on his name alone,
I don't trust him.
And I don't think you should either."

Clint is right, but not because his name
is Declan Lancaster III
although that part is in there too.
It's because he's a fake. Someone
who only wanted to date me
when I had everything. And now
that it's all gone,
so is he.

"Forget him," Clint says,
and I do.

All of a Sudden

I run through the field
clumsy and awkward,
trying to catch up with him,
the high grass scratching
my ankles. I can feel all
of summer around me.
The humid air beginning
to make me sweat, run
faster, get stronger. Most
of me is different than
before. Most of me more
free than I ever imagined
I would be. We skip
and jump through the field
and all of a sudden, we arrive
at the stable. The old farmhouse
big and run-down in the distance.

"You sure you're allowed
to come out here?" I ask.
Look around and the sky
feels wide and thick above us.
I feel out of place, like somehow
I am not supposed to be here,
like I am out of my element,
out of my comfort zone.
But as soon as he opens the door
and all of the horses come into
my view, I feel instantly at home.
There are two horses here
and I can't help but think

about my old stable and where
I used to ride. How much we needed,
how much we had. How much excess.
There was never ever enough to go
around. And once we had what we
needed, we always wanted more.

Clint is so gentle with the horses
that it makes me smile, makes me think
that maybe he could be this gentle
with me, and I didn't even know it,
didn't pay close enough attention
to him before now.

"Let's ride"

"What, you mean now?" I ask,
putting my palm to the horse.
"You sure it's okay?"

"Positive. This is Orange Crush
and this is Blackjack. Come on."

"Okay, but we need a saddle
and maybe just a longer intro, or . . ."

"Look, we can get all the information
or we can kinda be loose. Take a risk.
Go with Blackjack. He's a gamble."

I smile at Blackjack and then Clint.
Nod along and he helps me up.
No saddle. Nothing to protect me.
But maybe I've been closed off
my whole life. It's time to bet
and see where I land.

Clint whispers to both horses,
holds their faces in his hands.
Opens up the gate and then
eases up on Orange Crush
so the two of us are high up,
sitting on top of the countryside.
My stomach is tied up. Am I scared?
Of riding? Of feeling? Of crying?
Of letting totally loose? Of meeting
myself? Of trying to love for real?

Don't Think, Just Ride

So that's exactly what we do. Clint knows just what to say to these horses. They trust him, know him, respond to him, so when he hollers at them to run faster, they do. He knows this landscape, where we are, where we're going, I just hold on. Feel my heart start to pump faster, rougher, louder. Want to sing out too. Let him hear me. The ache and the let go. Don't want him to see the tears as they fall loose and wild from my eyes. I don't even wipe them away, just let it happen. What am I so scared of? The truth? Who I am underneath? With all that extra around me? What will happen if I just let go of the stuff? My ego? What people will think of me. *Go faster*, I think. And can feel my thighs hold on, my breath caught up. And suddenly it's not tears anymore, it's laughter, small at first just working to escape from my lungs, but then louder and bigger and it feels like I'm howling. Blackjack takes it to mean more and so he runs as fast as he can. Into the fields. So it looks like we are chasing sky and the fat clouds, and I throw my head back because what does it even matter anymore? What if I just said *let go* and then did exactly that. So that's what I do. See the risk and take it all the way home.

"Oh my god—what was that?"

Clint is laughing, shaking his head,
looking at me with some kind of awe.

"You just went wild up there, just
lost control and then got it back
and then lost it again. It was something
I don't see every day. That's for sure."

I smile back at him. Keep thinking
that every time I'm around him
I let go of something. But it's not
him. It's me. Shaking things off.
Letting myself do that unravel,
do that release that maybe I've
been needing for so long.

"Glad we got to hang today,"
he says, as we load the horses
back up. "I gotta head home,
but see you soon?"

The question lingers,
stays steady in the air,
but somehow, I do not
want to let him go
or this feeling every time
he is around me.

"No, no. We can't go yet.
We haven't even . . ." I look up,
"watched the sunset.

That seems like something
y'all do around here."

He laughs big now.
"You know what?
I feel like you're making fun,
but also, you are correct, we do that
so . . . let's go."

Sinking

It's not that I haven't ever seen
a sunset, but never like this,
never sprawled out in the grass
not caring about what's around us
or what could get us, scare us, make us
question our every decision. *Oh*, I think.
This is what it means to jump
without a net, or caution, or anyone
at all to catch you. I see it, feel it now.

Clint makes a star with his body,
a snow angel but in the grass. Here we are
out in the country. The fireflies are out
and I wanna run to catch them,
but Clint lays perfectly still. His body calm.

"We don't have to go anywhere," he says.

So I don't move either. My muscles calm.
Sore, but quiet. Look up at the sky.
It's not fireworks, but feels like
it might as well be. Since my stomach
is flipping and jutting. Turning and bumping.

Clint's hand touches mine for a second
and my whole body feels like sky too.
Vast, never-ending. Deep and intense.

Just the feel of his skin next to mine
sends my whole heart on flight.
And I've never felt this with anyone else.

Ever. I fall asleep on his shoulder
so when the sun wakes us up I'm shocked
to still be outside with him. His body tucked
and curled beside me. Mapping us,
imprinting us.

"I have to go home," Clint
whispers. "For real this time."

He looks at me, sleepy. Then up
toward the light coming on.

"Last night felt like a dream," he says.

Just Like a Dream

But after Clint leaves
and I wake up,
I realize everything
I used to know
and love is still gone.
Can't stop thinking
about what it means
to lose all
I've ever known.
That old life
left behind.
Still angry
at my dad
and mom.
Still reeling,
still confused,
still lost,
still lonely,
still scared,
still questioning,
still can't answer
my own questions
without feeling like
I have all the wrong
answers.

The truth is—

having money
makes you feel
powerful,
in control,
beautiful.
Makes you feel
all on top
of the world,
on top
of the planet.

A star.

Having money
makes you feel
unbeatable,
unstoppable,
invincible.

Yeah, yeah.
That's the way
it does
magic to you.

Makes you feel
all types of
fantastical,
phenomenal,
all electrical,
nonstoppable.

My truth is—

having money
has made me look
at other people
with a kind of
side eye. Like
they're not good
enough. If they
don't have enough.
If they are not worth
enough. I know this
is true for me. True
for who I used to be.
But I don't want to be
that girl anymore.
I am sick of the past,
of the me that was always
looking down on everyone
else. Now it's time
to look closer
at myself.

Not having money

comes with shame,
comes with dread,
comes with fear
and anxiety.
And I don't want
that to be the only story,
the only conversation
that anyone has.

What if I looked
at this situation,
at my life,
at this place,
with a different
kind of lens?

With something
like
tenderness
or softness
or love.

Reframe

Next day, I see Clint straight away
and try to pretend I know what I am doing
with all my free time. Also try to cover up
the fact that I cannot get him out
from my mind.

Clint looks right at me, calls me over.
"I got the whole day free. You look like
you need a break. Let's go downtown."

My mom has all but disappeared in meetings
with lawyers and going to visit my dad,
who I can't bring myself to face yet. Still, I'm alone.

"Yeah. I'd like that," I say, thinking I would.
"But I don't have any money." I realize
that anything I really want to do
will require us to be spending all day.
I think about what we used to do after school.
How we would drive to get coffee, then cruise
all the shops, grab food,
order anything we wanted off the menus.
Money was nothing at all to me then.

"I bet I can show you a good time
with no money at all," Clint says.

"No way. I just don't believe it."

"Yeah, that's because you clearly
have no creativity! Come on.

You gotta see things in a big way,
pull the camera back and see
bigger than yourself. See wider.
Look. Just trust me.
You think you can do that?"

And I do not have an answer
just yet. Swallow some or most
of my pride right on down.

"Fine. I trust you. Kind of.
And also, I just wanna get out
of here. So let's go. Are you
gonna drive?"

"You really know nothing about me, do you?"

Clint asks and looks around the parking lot.
"What exactly do you think I drive?
And where do you think my car is?"
He starts to look frantically around
like he's searching, trying to find it.
"You think somebody stole it? Thieves!"

I look around for his car for real now,
since Mom has ours,
but look up and he's laughing.
I get the feeling he never had a car
in the first place. I am always the joke.
All I see is a beat-up old bike
leaned up against his apartment.

"Come on. You can ride with me," he says
trying to stop laughing, holding the bike up.

"I'm sorry, on what?" I ask.
He points to the pegs on the side.

"Are you joking? I can't balance on that.
You really don't have a car? You have to have a car."

"No, see that's the thing, we don't all
have to have cars. That's just a big ole lie
that someone like Declan tells people.
I mean I bet *Declan* has a car,
but that's prolly just 'cause
he can't really ride a bike,
which is really sad to me."

"You got jokes, huh?"

"All day. Come on. Jump on."

Suddenly, I want out

Standing there trying to figure out
how I am going to get out of this
conversation, this day, this whole
experiment that's called having fun
without spending any money,
which I am positive is not a real thing.

"Chloe, I am gonna need you to calm
all the way down. You don't need
to get all keyed up about five miles.
It'll take about thirty minutes—max.
I mean, we're seventeen years old
so we're kind of in the best shape
of our lives. You get that, right?
You could prolly jog beside me
and be there in less than twenty."

"I am not jogging, okay? Have we
even met? I do not jog. And what
am I supposed to wear anyway?
I can't wear tennis shoes to go out,
I mean—I wanna look good,
I wanna look the way . . ."

"What way? I don't understand.
Is there a certain way you gotta look?"

I don't respond, just stare straight at Clint.

"All right, well whatever that look is,
forget about all that.

Just let that go. Wear sneakers.
Or hell, even flip-flops.
Just wear what feels right.
You don't gotta be all fancy,
that's all I'm saying.
This is what I'm gonna wear.
Just be comfortable. We're not
going anywhere too fancy anyhow.
Just lemme show you a good time,"
he finishes. And the way he says it,
and the way he's standing in front of me
with the sun beginning to shine hot
and wide in the sky above us
makes me wanna go everywhere
with him.

"Are you sure it's safe?"

I ask, looking from the rusty handlebars
to the pegs where he is pointing for me to hop on.

"I mean, what's safe in the world anyway?"

"That is not an answer."

"I don't have one. What I'm saying
is that everything in life is a risk."

"That's so philosophical."

"I try." He smiles. "Come on. Take a risk."

I take a deep breath and let it out slow.

"I'll go slow. I swear it. Don't be scared."

I cover my face with my hands
because life feels embarrassing
and thrilling all at the same time
and I want to ride with Clint
all over downtown even if I'm broke.
I wanna exist with him.
Hang and just be with him.
When I close my eyes
I can't stop thinking of him.

"Come on," he says, "let's ride."

And So We Do

I stand on the pegs in the back
of the bike, and he sits in front of me.
"Just hold on to my shoulders," he says,
and I lean down into his hair
that smells clean and just washed,
and I want to bury my face there but stop.
"Hold on tight, okay?"
And then he looks up at me, right there
into my eyes. And suddenly, I want to kiss him,
stay there on the back of the bike with him,
stay in this moment forever with him,
forgetting about my past and knowing
the future doesn't exist the way I thought
it did. I want to hold on to this,
and then we're off. The wind
washing soft against my face
as he pulls out of the rocks
and onto the backcountry roads
that lead us from the apartment
to downtown. All of Kentucky
feels clear and wide open, the hills
that rise and dip around us,
all the green that lasts forever.
The picket fences
and the stone fences too.
All the history spread out before me,
all the stories I've been told,
every single moment held close.
Let the air flow through me.
Close my eyes and hold on tighter.
I can feel Clint tense beneath my palms.
And it makes me want to hold on forever.

"You good?"

he calls back at me
and I holler back "Yes."

He takes all the dips and turns,
leads us right straight downtown.

"Here we are," he says,
and pauses so I can jump off.

"See how easy that was?"

"Yeah. I didn't die.
I'm really thankful for that."

He laughs and gets off too.
We are standing near the courthouse
and I start to look at all the buildings,
some of which have our name on them.

"So what's the plan?" I ask, still
not believing we can have fun
and not spend any money at all.

"Well, we gotta eat, right?
Come on. I got you."

The Dairy Bar

We walk inside and the smell of grease
and burgers spills out onto everything.
I realize I am starving, having eaten cereal
all week long. Customers are lined up
at the bar and everyone says hi to Clint.

"Wait, do you work here?" I ask.
"That's not fair."

"Look, I got some favors to call in.
Be right back," he says, smiling.

He shows me to a booth and disappears
inside the back of the kitchen. I take it in.
This is a place we'd sometimes come late night
after drinking or hanging downtown. A dive.
We'd always make fun of the smell,
how it would ruin all of our clothes.

When Clint comes back, he brings me
iced hot chocolate mixed with coffee
and it feels like I could drink it all afternoon.
A few minutes later, a bowl of steaming grits
with pieces of bacon broken up inside.
Fried eggs and sauteed kale with garlic and onions
and the whole place feels like a kind of heaven.
Sweet and savory all at the same time.

"And what about when the check comes?" I ask.

"Debbie, how much did you say this was?"
Clint calls out to the woman behind the counter.

"It's on the house, honey. You know we got you,"
she says. I look at Clint.

"No, no. This is so suspect. What, you're just
gonna call in all your favors like that?"

"It's all about the relationships.
That's the difference I'm talking about.
A little give, a little take.
It's on the house, honey," he says
repeating what Debbie said
and it sounds both smooth and corny
coming from Clint.

I Love It Here

The jukebox is in the corner
and Clint says if you kick it just right
it'll add free songs, so that's what he does
and tells me to choose three to play.
I walk to the music and scroll through.
It should be easy, but with only three songs
you have to choose wisely. I study close,
then put Tina Turner on heavy rotation
with "Private Dancer" and "I Can't Stand the Rain"
and then I go to Willie Nelson and Dolly Parton
and imagine what Clint would choose. Country.
Wonder what his country playlist would include
and want to make sure I play something
that will stay with him, that will stay with both of us
long after I play it.

Transformational vs. Transactional

"That's what I'm working on. Relationships,"
Clint says again. We're walking down the street
having just finished the biggest meal of my life.

"What I mean is that it's all about getting to know
people. Not always asking for everything.
I'm not all the time trying to transact with people.
I give them something and they give me something
back. Transactional is always getting something
in return. But transformational is different.
It changes you. Changes the people you meet.
It's basically how I got us free breakfast," he says.

"Yeah, yeah, but transactional is not all bad,"
I say, walking past my favorite boutique. I stop
and stare into the window—longing for everything
that I see. "Sometimes you give just so you can receive.
For instance, I want that dress right there,
and if I give the salesperson my money
she wraps it up in beautiful paper
and hands it to me in a gold bag.
I know this because I have been here . . ."

"Chloe, is that you?"

The door opens and the exact salesperson
I was talking about is standing in front of me. "Oh my god!
We have missed you and your mom sooo much!
We have sooo many gowns that would be so perfect
for you and all this new jewelry that's coming in,
and, oh my god, I just cannot believe what is happening."

She pulls me into a hug and Clint stands back to watch.

"Oh, wow. Thank you, it's so good to see you too.
I'm sorry, I am just . . . We're in a little bit of a hurry, so . . ."

"Oh, oh, sorry. Yeah, I totally understand. It's just . . .
well . . . Also one other thing . . . We have been calling
and reaching out . . . It's just . . . there is a, umm . . . a bill
that hasn't been paid yet, so could you . . . talk with
your dad or your mom or your . . ."

I start to nod furiously. Panicked, realizing Clint
still doesn't know anything about me or us.

"Yes! Absolutely. I am so on it. I will let Mom know!"

"I don't wanna talk about it,"
I state. We are on the corner.
Staring at each other. "Not today."

"Cool. Not my business," he replies.
"Besides, we got some free shit to do."

And at that, we're off.

First stop

is the library. It's cool and smells clean.

The books all laid out in perfect rows.
It makes me forget the money we owe.

We go to the picture books and he shares
his favorites from when he was a kid.

We read sections to each other. Travel
to poetry and history, fiction and magazines.

I show him my favorite fall looks. Long
for all of it. Listen in at story time too.

Head to the fancy hotel & art museum,
spend an hour looking at paintings,

then sculptures and designs. Take a walk
through the gardens blooming in the back.

Listen to a musician play jazz on the corner.
Music and art and books and the whole day

feels full. I stay shocked that Clint managed
to get my whole mind to let go of the past.

I Trust Him—I Do

At the end of the day, we sit outside
right on the steps in front of the fountain.

"This is actually my favorite show right here.
I used to come down with my pop
every Fourth of July and they'd do fireworks
and we'd all run around in the fountain.
Ever since he died, every time I come down
it makes me think of him."

I am about to ask him about his dad
when he looks at me and says,
"I don't wanna talk about it."

I nod and change the subject.
"It is hot as hell out here," I say.
"Maybe we should just go back
before I start to melt. Besides,
I'm too sticky and hot to do anything else.
And you're right. You proved it.
This day has been sooo good.
Now we can just go back
and sit in front of a fan
or something like that?"

"No. I can't let you leave yet.
Come on," he says, and all of a sudden
he is taking off his shoes. One at a time.
Unlacing both sneakers, and then pulling off his socks too.
Wiggling his toes in front of me,
stretching out and taking up space.

"What are you doing?" I ask.

"We're gonna cool off. You.
Need to cool off. Come on."

Catch Me

Clint peels his shirt off,
so quick, so easy, I catch
my breath. *Oh, he looks like that.*
Underneath his shirt. Oh my god.
He speeds toward
all the water shooting up,
up into the sky. Raining,
exploding. Rushes right in.
Unexpected. Wild.
He calls to me.
Yells at me to join
and so I do. Keep
all my clothes on,
but get drenched
in the spray.
He pulls me
so close I can
feel his breath
at my neck
and the cool
wetness
surrounds
me.

I almost
forget
the
past.

At home, panic sets in

I find a way to push it all behind,
but once Clint drops me off,
my anger starts to rise up.

"Mom, Mom! Where are you?"

"In the bedroom, sweetie.
What's up?" She walks out.
"Why are you soaked?
What have you been up to?"

"Clint and I jumped in the fountain.
It's no big deal. But what is, is that
I was at the Bluegrass Boutique today."

 "Why in the world did you go there?"

"No, I didn't go there, I was outside of it
and Melanie came to say hi and tell me
how much she missed me and you—us!"

"Well, that's very nice of her."

"That's not the point, Mom. The point
is that we have unpaid bills. And no one
is returning their calls, so could you . . . ?"

"It's okay, honey. We just have to default.
That's all."

"That is not okay. Not at all.
How can you . . . be so calm about it all?"

"You think I am calm?" Mom's voice goes up.
But she's not yelling. "I am furious.
I am lost and alone here. Without
your dad, without our home,
most of the time without you.
I am only pretending to be calm.
I am just as scared as you are."
Then her voice gets louder.
"Don't tell me how I feel.
And don't start a fight you can't finish,"
Mom yells, suddenly grabbing her purse
and trying to walk away.

I Stop Her

Mom is a tornado,
careening,
whooping,
posing,
prancing.

I am an avalanche,
crashing,
sliding,
sinking,
exploding.

Can't catch up.
Can't catch my breath.

"You are the mom!" I shout back.
"You can't just turn our lives off
and then back on again
like some stoplight.
We don't just go on command."
She reaches the door.
"This is real life, Mom.
You have to remember
who you were before.
Bring her back.
The one in here
cooking corn bread
and singing
all off-key
and silly.
Not this one.

The one acting
like nothing is wrong.
Things are wrong,"
I start to cry.
"Really, really wrong.
And if you can't admit it,
if you won't even try,
then how am I supposed to learn?
How am I supposed to even live?"

Mom Is Gone and I Miss My Father

Miss him the most in moments like this.
Miss the way he would make things right,
fix anything that was broken.
He did it with money mostly,
but with connections too—
the kind of relationships
Clint was talking about today.
He had them—everywhere.
But I am starting to see parts of him
I tried to keep tucked away.
I am beginning to see his failures,
and I am trying to be forgiving
and trying to hold on to who
I thought he was,
but every day some new story
plays out in front of me.

He was all about
the transactions.
Give and take.

I miss my father
but I am starting to notice
he was more complicated
than I knew, or thought I knew.
I miss his presence
and his every day,
miss how he would make me shine.
I miss his shine
and the way he lit everyone up
when he was around.

I miss the way Mom was
with him. All lit up too. Alive.
I miss him the most
when I'm trying to remember
who I was before he left.

REMEMBERING THE PAST

Alone Again

I remember this feeling too.
The being left behind.
The loneliness.

Saying good night to them
before another benefit
or gala or work event.

The busyness, filling our time,
the never enough, racing up,
the accumulating, the spending.

We could never have enough.
Dad swore the more we had
the easier it would be.

And it was. But the excess
meant too much work, meant
stress, anxiety, sleepless nights.

They fought over my life,
school choices, activities,
summer camps, extracurriculars.

I was meant to help make them
accomplished, proud, poised.
Felt that same pressure for perfection.

So I crammed, I studied, I styled,
I shopped, I craved, I wanted,
I bought, I consumed, I needed.

The more we made, the more we spent,
the more we spent, the more we made,
the more we made, the more we spent.

A cycle we couldn't get enough of.
Run ragged by. One I am still trying
to get away from.

Try to Remember

All the good.
Laughter late at night
around the kitchen table,
hearing stories, watching
the way he loved Mom,
her voice, her style, the way
she could put anyone at ease.

"Sing for us," Dad would say,
and I would. Unafraid, bold.

"Play for us. Perform. Read us
your new lyrics. What do you dream
about in this life?" he would ask.

Such a miracle to be asked to dream
and then given all the gifts to just
make it happen. I see that now.

Showcase. Show off. Stunt. Spectacle.
A whole life dedicated to the stage,
the performance, the presentation.

Watch what I can do. That's the way
Mom lived too. Pageant. Parade. Ornate.
The way she'd flaunt, flash, flourish for all.

What do we do now that no one is watching?
Without all the grandstanding? Nothing to boast
or brag about? It's just us.

How will we live now?

Mom Comes Back

"I had to get these out of storage,"
she says. "Figured it was important
enough for you to see."

And her arms are loaded
with photo albums, letters,
and what look like journals
full of cursive handwriting
that I've never seen before.

She spreads them over the floor,
opens each book to photos
of her as a baby right here,
pulling tomatoes off the vine
and digging her toes in dirt.

Big group shots at the same
picnic tables that're outside.
Watermelon and fried catfish,
faces smiling wide, gleaming
heads thrown back laughing.

Lana Brooks at fifteen and eighteen.
Looking like she knows all.
Posing, playing, showing off.
Happy to be here, not trying
to be anything else at all.

Portraits of Mom

Each photo, the smiles are wider than the next.
In one, her hair is wild around her face, no front teeth,
standing on the swing, holding the chains
and about to take off into the sky.

Then with her mom and dad at the picnic table.
Feast spread out before them. Fried chicken,
collards, plate full of biscuits. Energy around them,
kids everywhere. Mom holding a sparkler in her hand,
the sun setting behind them. Grass manicured,
grounds kept clean and fresh.

In every picture, the apartments behind her
are freshly painted, the trim neat and polished.
Granny and Papaw holding her up as a baby
and then arms holding on to her as a kid.
All of them crowded around family and friends.
Limestone Apartments was clearly the place to be.

There she is again. All grown up.
Riding a horse and laughing. Full of energy,
fire, and grit. Cutoff jeans frayed and loose.
Torn T-shirt. Hair thrown up in a messy knot.
Not caring. Looks like she could be Clint's sister.
All cool and confident. Looking fierce, steady.
Unstoppable. And it makes me see myself too.

Next, it's Lana Jones—her maiden name.
Ms. Fayette County splashed over her,
glittering crown on her head, hair in waves,

in curls. All Kentucky styled. Southern.

Mom used to say, "Kentucky girls have horsehair. At least the prettiest ones do." She certainly did.

The Next Albums

She pulls out the ones from their early days.
Just meeting, just married, just rising up
in the world. Just starting to make money,
just starting to make a name for themselves.
There they are. Mom and Dad and every pose
remains the same. On his arm, by his side,
small smile, subdued. Show the teeth,
but not too many. There is no laughing,
no let go, no messy around the edges.
There's pulled together, don't let them
see you sweat or cringe or shake. Pristine.

She had to fit into a world she didn't belong to.
Where in the world does she belong now?

Look Through the Past

Mom's journals lay out on the floor.
She opens them up and poems
or songs or lyrics, or just
whatever was in her head
spreads out before us.

She reads them aloud to me.
Doesn't sing them, but she might
as well. They are music, they are free.

Love Story

Love me all the way. Each time.
Every word I say. Love me plain
and love me deep. What I want.
What I'm ready for. See me simple.
Not a fantasy. Not filtered
or photoshopped, not smoothed out
or sharpened up. See me makeup-free.
See me the way I arrived. Ready to love me
without all that extra too.

Kentucky Sky

All of me is wind, winding, shadow, dawn.
All of me is hillsides, mountaintops, gone.

Most of me is homesick, crying for the past.
Most of me is lonesome, heart is all but crashed.

So I go outside to reach inside, all of me is sky.
So I go outside to reach inside, all of me goodbye.

Bluegrass raised me up to see another side of me.
Bluegrass raised me up to see, the best part is we.

"Mom, explain yourself!"

"What are these? And why
am I only just seeing them now?"

Mom closes her eyes, leans
her head all the way back.
Breathes in and out. I wait.

"Just something I used to love.
Writing, singing. Playing," she says.
"You knew I played piano
and guitar. That's what I wanted
for you. Why I always pushed you."

"Because you didn't follow it
yourself." She nods.

"By the time I met your dad,
I was focused on other things.
On looking perfect and acting
perfect and presenting perfect
to the world. It's what he wanted.
But it's what I wanted too.
It was both of us. And that
is what we wanted for you.
It was a mistake."

She says this part quiet.
Because it's a truth
neither one us
wants to admit.

Mom Keeps On

"What if everything I thought I knew
was wrong? All the things I believed
would make life better.
If all the parts of me were false.
Made up. Make believe.
What if all I imagined to be true
was a lie? What then?
Who would I be then?
It was just stuff—just excess.
Just clothes and jewelry and furniture.
My dad, your papaw was all the time saying,
You can't take it with you. That's how I was raised.
To think that stuff didn't matter. It didn't make you.
So how did I get so caught up in those lies?
And now there is nothing left to take
even if we wanted to.
What does it even mean to lose everything?
How am I supposed to love myself
now that it's all gone?"

We Call Dad

We have to.
Hear his voice.
Cry for home.
Hold each other.
He breaks down.
So do we.
Say we're hurt.
Say we're grieving.
Let anger out.
Say we're sorry.
Calm each other.
Try to forgive.
Somehow, some way.

WHO ARE WE NOW?

Outside

The crew is all sitting together.
Of course, they heard the fight.
Of course, they are in on it all.
Of course, they have no idea
who I really am or what I stand for.
I don't know that either.
Just trying to figure that out.

"Come on over. Join us.
You can tell them how I proved
that you don't need money
to have a good time," Clint says,
his hair still wet, clothes too.

And suddenly, I want someone
to take it out on. Just like my mom
took it out on me.

"It's bullshit, okay? You do
need money. Everyone does.
It was fine for the day. Yeah,
we had fun, but you need cash.
You gotta pay bills and cover
expenses. You gotta eat, right?"

They all stay steady looking at me.
I can't help myself. I go on, go off.

"I don't belong here"

"Sorry, I don't.
This is not who I am," I say,
looking around at the mess,
leaving out the part
that it's my family's fault.
"This is not my home.
Not this crappy apartment
or this trashy complex.
This land is not mine."
I find myself shouting,
clearly still not okay
with this or anything
happening. Go on
and wipe the tears
and slow down
tell myself to stop
the anger
from
rising.

Not Our Land

"I'm just saying. This land
is definitely not our land.
So you can forget about that.
You can forget about owning
anything at all. This is stolen
land. Taken land," Skye says,
not paying attention to my fit,
to my tantrum that is breaking
whatever trust I'd tried to build.

"Okay, whatever," I say.
"I'm just saying this place
that you all call home.
This is not my home."

"Right. And what I am saying,
what we are saying, is that this
land is not ours to own.
Maybe you're used to owning
things, but that's not
what we're about."

"This is Shawnee, Cherokee,
Chickasaw, and Osage land.
This has never been our land,"
Clint says, leaning back again.

"Oh," I say, suddenly realizing
what they are saying. "I didn't,
I didn't realize what you meant.
I'm . . . sorry about that. I just
meant it's not mine. That's all."

"It's not ours either," Clint says,
and walks over to the fence,
his face tilting up to the sky.

None of this is even something
I would ever think about. My mind
feels at a loss for real now. Feels all
bumped about and jumbled in my head.

I sit

slumped down on the fold-out chair beside them.
They don't welcome me to the table again.

"Oh," I say. "I get it. I'm sorry," I admit.
"I got a lot going on. I shouldn't have said any of that."

"You're from Kentucky too, you know?" Clint says,
leaning back even farther and looking at me steady now.

"I never said I wasn't. I'm not trying to . . . I know,"
I say again, tumbling over my own words. "I know."

"So then start acting like it. Stop pretending
you're so different or so much better than us.
You walk around here like you own the place."

I stay quiet. Do not tell him that we do own it.
That my father has betrayed us and our whole life
is a lie that I keep on trying to tell.

"Look, we don't know what your whole story is,
but long as you're gonna be here, you might need
to change it up a little. Cool off a bit," Natalia adds.

"You think we need to go jump in the fountain again?"
Clint asks. "Or maybe just the old-fashioned water hose?"

And when he says it, he goes to turn on the hose
and sprays it up into the air.

"Everyone needs to just cool off"

"and calm the hell down," Clint says.
What is with this kid?

Clint holds the hose into the air.
Sprays it loose above him.
A firecracker of water rains.
Not a care. About image.
What he looks like. What we
look like to him. He smiles.
James and Skye hold their arms
out toward the clouds. Natalia
jumps and waves. Dodging
or welcoming the chaos.
They are not afraid of anything.

Why have I been living my life
so closed up, closed off. Worried
about every small part of me.
Not letting all of me show up?

Lose Control

That's what we do.
Suddenly running,
dodging, jumping,
sweating, hollering,
lunging, breathing,
breaknecking,
flying, floating,
bouncing, laughing,
out-of-controlling,
let going, mind
blowing, body
loosening, not
worrying, stop
caring, quit
regulating,
restraining,
can't catch
us. Free.

We are bodies
running wild.

Running Turns to Singing

And I can't tell if these kids
are for real. But I don't care.
I don't know the words,
but start to hum too.
And just like laughing
while riding Blackjack
and just like letting Mom
cry for her past and reading
her poems and songs,
I want to be unexpected.
I want to be worthy.
Of love, trust.
Not just worth things
and excess and stuff.
But worthy of love.
Worthy of the truth.
So I let my voice go
higher and stronger.
Let it reach deeper
and truer.

They Stop, Stare at Me

"Oh my god. I'm sorry.
I don't even know the words.
I just got caught up.
That was weird. Never mind."

"We didn't even say anything,"
James says. "But you got a voice."

I smile. Thankful he heard it.
Thankful to be part of something.

"Yeah, I . . . love singing. And music.
Writing music actually. I was gonna
spend my whole summer working on it,
but now that's all over, so . . ."

"What do you mean?" James asks
pushing further.

"I was just supposed to go to this summer
program to learn a bunch of stuff,
but that's done. Not happening.
My whole life kinda
feels like it's finished."

The Sky Goes Dark

I break it all down. Open up.
Don't stay silent any longer.

"I had my whole life planned out.
The whole thing. Just so you know.
And now my family is going through it
and they can't totally afford to send me
or to let me do any of the things I planned."

Clint doesn't respond. Just stares out.
Doesn't even look at me. Just up, up.

But I keep on. "What I mean is that
everything was set up for me. My life.
Going to Europe then LA.
Music production. Recording,
writing songs, getting in the studio. That's it.
That's what I want to do with my life.
Make music. Learn from the best people
in the best city. But now I am stuck right here."

"So you think there's no music here?"

Clint asks, and he looks around at everyone
and they all break out laughing. Their voices
all of a sudden sounding like a song,
but one I do not want to hear.

"Are you making fun of me?" I ask,
but already know the answer.
Feel like such a fake. Feel like such a poser.

"Nah, nah, we're not making fun of *you*,"
Clint says. "Come on. You gotta hear yourself.
It's like you've traveled all over the world,
seen all kinds of things,
prolly speak another language or two,
but you're not seeing what's right here
in front of you. Look," he says, holds up his hand
and points out toward the fields and the sky,
reaches over to the stables and stands up
to catch a firefly between his palms.

"If you don't start looking around here
and listening and paying attention to this,
to us, to your life . . . then you're gonna miss it.
You're gonna miss the whole thing."

History Lesson

"Look, Chloe, you are all caught up
in what everybody else thinks you should do.
The places everybody says you gotta go.
None of that even matters. None of it.
What if you just focused on here.
On now. On us. What we do.
You wanted to be our manager, remember?
You could join us too. Hang with us.
Sing with us. Oh, and clog with us,"
Skye says, holds her finger up,
says to wait one second
and comes back with a pair of clogs
that look like the ones Mom unpacked
earlier today. "You clog?" she asks.

I shake my head no, but this all feels so Kentucky
for real. The *click clack* of Skye dancing.
Natalia's alto. Clint's rumble. James
keeping the beat, the bass line.

The we don't care.
The no one tells us.
The listen or don't.
The confidence.
The royalty.
Bravado.
Ego.
The middle finger
to the sky.
The cocky.
The smirk.

They got it all,
and I want
to be
part
of
it
too.

They Sing

And the way all of their voices
braid together stops me.
A thread, linked
and moving as one.
I want to listen to them
all night long.

Forget the past, any trouble
that feels like it's following me.
Let it all go. And sing
along
with them.
So finally,
I do.

Look, come on now.
You gotta just dance.
Just feel it.
Just rock it.
Don't stop it.
Oh yeah.

That's it.
Just move.
Just free.
Just loose.
Just yes.

Music

The tambourine comes out
and Skye sings louder
and then me too.
Let it all flow loose
and easy.
Throw my head back,
let loose my whole body
and just flow
and just go
and just free.
Free.
Free.
Not worried
about the past
or my life
before this.
I get it.
Don't have to prove,
show it.
Just own it,
just be it.
Just see it,
just dream it,
just make
it happen.
That's what they do.

Past Tense

My people were rich.
That's all I thought there was to it.
That was the end of the story.
All that ever mattered.
My dad and his people
and their people
and all the people
who came before.

This Kentucky
is not the home
I am used to.

My language
is a rich kid's language.
My language
is a type of luxury.
It is business class
and I hate myself for it.

Having money meant
we were full of goodness.
Having money
meant we were smart
and wholesome.

It meant we won.
We made it.
And now
that it's gone.

What does that say
about us
now?

Where I Come From

Who I come from. All of it matters.
All the ways we exist in the world.
I was always taught to be the star of the show,
the main attraction, and now I am somewhere else,
somewhere on the margins and left behind.
Somewhere they can't see me anymore,
can't seem to find me anymore.
Clint and Skye keep talking about all the people
who came before us and how this land
is not really our land. A kind of history
I have never been taught.
A history that was left behind. Left out.
Whose story is fit for the telling?
My father always had a hierarchy
of who was most important,
and it wasn't the people who came before us,
and it's none of the new people I am hanging with.
They would not have landed on his list.
His list that grew and grew
and started to leave out all the people my mom came from.
My mother was there too—decorating
and making her house shine fantastic.
Ignoring the destruction. Ignoring the broken
and left behind. Keeping her eyes closed to the deceit.
But I guess in a way, I did the same thing.
Chose not to look or question my situation.
As long as things were good, as long as I had everything
I could ever want or need, then things were fine.
My life was a prize I had won.

There is a distance now.

Misconceptions. Ideas about a place.

Know I need to break out
of who I am
and who I was supposed to be.

New Day

The next morning, I get up when the sun does.
All pouring thick into my bedroom window.

My mom does not even stir. Stays steady, still.
Get up to make my own bed, roll to the kitchen.

Pour myself a bowl of cereal. Eat it alone,
staring out the window. Last night changed me.

Last night felt alive and energized. Last night
I felt different than I ever have and want more.

I splash water on my face and don't worry
about makeup or making myself look different.

Barely have time to look in the mirror
and am outside at the picnic tables. Waiting.

Fifteen minutes turns into forty-five. I pick up my phone
and start to text Clint, but don't know what to say.

Look over to Clint's place. And then to Natalia's
and to James's and Skye's. It seems impossible they're sleeping.

So I walk to the front of Clint's apartment
and go ahead and ring the doorbell. Then knock.

No one is home. Anywhere. All apartments
look shut up and closed down. Silent.

Alone

Nothing around me.
No noise, no voices.
No alerts or notifications.

I sit alone on the table.
Think about last night.
The let go, the ease, calm.

Close my eyes and push
away the fear. The stranded,
the panic. Try to stay steady.

I miss the way Dad would fill
all those quiet spaces. His over
the top, his ego. But he is gone.

"No one was home"

This is how I start the conversation.
Clint, Skye, James, and Natalia appear
around six p.m. Hanging, talking,
laughing loud. Rowdy.

"Uh, yeah, no one was home
because we work," Clint says,
looking at me like he's just seeing me.

"Like an internship?"

"You mean one of those jobs where they don't pay you?
That's the kind of thing you mean?" Skye asks and laughs.

I nod. Every time I start to talk about my life before this
I feel like a complete fool.

"The answer is no. We do not do internships.
That is for rich kids who do not need money to pay
for things. Like food or clothes or a bike or car."

I do not respond. I have started to feel like all my answers
sound brainwashed in a way. Or maybe not brainwashed
but clouded over. Unaware.

We All Have Jobs

"We all got paying jobs that is.
I love mine. You saw all that free food.
They love me too. Hard not to."
He smiles, shows all his teeth.
I am starting to really see why.
He is somehow irresistible
with all that positivity.
"You said it—nothing in life is free.
Don't you know that?
You gotta have money
for rent and clothes
and what else did you say yesterday?"
he asks.

"All I know is you do get free food,
but you also stink like grease
every single day," Natalia adds in.
"Seriously, you smell so bad."

They all start to laugh and Clint
leans his head toward me,
his hair right up close to my face
to smell him. And I do.
And they're right. He smells like French fries,
and sweat too. And the combination
makes me dizzy.

"What do the rest of you do?"

I ask. Looking around the table now.

"Goodwill," Natalia and James say.
"That's why I got all the best looks—
'cause I basically get to rifle through
a bunch of clothes and stuff that people
just get rid of. Just toss away like it's nothing.
And I also get a discount."

She high-fives James who looks like
the most fashionable one in the group.

"We don't buy anything new.
None of us do. This is all thrift.
Actually Clint only wears like three things, so . . ."

"What is that? Is that supposed to make me feel bad?
Because it doesn't. It's called a uniform.
It's called setting up your priorities.
In some circles it is called genius,
so you can just use that if you would like," Clint says.

"And what about you, Skye? What do you do?"

"Well, first of all, Skye is a lyricist. She writes all our songs.
So she's gotta be working on that most of the time,"
Natalia says, clearly Skye's hype crew.

"But I got a job too. At the Lexington Public Library.
I do story time and help with programming
and reading with the kids. That kind of thing.

To be honest, it's kind of like an internship.
I was, uh . . . nominated."

I smile this time. "So should I get a . . . job?" I ask.
They all look at me and start laughing again.
This is becoming a pattern. I talk. They laugh.

"A job is not a dirty word"

Natalia says this, standing up now. Walking over
to the bulletin board with all the listings on it.

"No, I know. You're right. I've just never had one.
I mean I thought in college I would get
an internship or something to do
that would help my resume or whatever.
But I could do a job."

They start to laugh again,
every time I open my mouth.
"It's not funny," I say.

"We're not laughing at you.
We're just laughing at the situation," Clint says,
coming over to sit beside me and bringing his smell
and his energy and this whole can't stop thinking of him
vibe over with him.

"We know you can work. We know you can get a job.
But do you really want one? If you get a *job* job,
that means you gotta stay the whole summer."

"Well, I don't really have anywhere else to go, so . . ."

"My voice is my ticket"

This is what Skye says
right at the end of the night.

Natalia and Clint say good night.
Both have to get up early for their shifts.

Everyone says, "I love you. I love you."
to each other before heading home.

It's just me, Skye, and James left
watching all the stars get brighter.

Her voice is beacon and shine.
I want to stay a stretch longer.

"You mean outta Kentucky?"
I want to know where she will go.

"No, I love this state. The Bluegrass
is home to me. Always will be."

"Then where? What do you mean?"
I want to know her place, her plans.

"I mean outta this trash apartment."

I look around and know she is right.
Sometimes it feels abandoned.

As if everyone forgot it existed.
As if we all shut the door on it.

But I look at Skye and James,
remember people are still here.

Their whole lives and dreams.
What they want, wish for.

Skye says

"I always dream I'm in a place
that I feel proud of. Not too fancy."
I want a place I can call home.
One I want to invite folks back to.
You know what I mean?"

I do. I know our home
was a place where everyone
wanted to be. Always clean,
always welcoming. Everything
up-to-date. Manicured. Polished.
Always fresh. Always gleaming.

I am embarrassed and so full of shame
that we've let this place
get so far away from who we are,
or who we thought we were.

Community and Love Right Here

"Every time we think about leaving,
we think about everybody who lives here,"
James says, following behind Skye and her words.
"These are our people, so even if the place
is struggling, the community makes it
what it is."

"James is easily the most loving person
on the planet," Skye says.
"He can find the beauty
in every single thing.
It's his and Clint's superpower.
I don't know how they do it.
Natalia and I like to bring the reality.
But those two. Dreamers for sure."
Skye pulls him toward her for a hug.

Focus on the Divine

"That's what our granny used to say, right,"
James asks and Skye nods along.

"I don't wanna get caught up in the past
or what didn't happen or what might've been.
I stay right here. And I got dreams too, you know.
Skye might wanna stay here, but I got New York City
on my mind. All the time. A place here in the country
and then some high-rise apartment designing clothes
for the group, for musicians. You know. Falling in love."

"What'd I say? The most loving, the most crush-having,
the fastest one to fall in love." Skye raises her eyebrows.

"I love love. What can I say? My heart is open.
I'm not gonna say that Lil Nas X and I are exclusive,
but I do love him a lot. I am also feeling Harry Styles
even though I know he's not totally my type.
But I'm just saying, love is where it's at.
Course you, Mama, and Daddy are my first loves.
You know that," James says,
planting a kiss on Skye's cheek.

Speaking of Love

"So you like Clint, huh?" James asks,
just before we head inside. End the night.

"What? No, I . . . I didn't . . . I never said . . .
What do you mean? I don't . . . What?"
What am I even saying? "He's cool."
Ahhh, that is even worse.

"You can admit it. He's got something, right?
Everybody loves him. And he's for real,"
James says. "Been knowing Clint since first grade.
Been with him through growing up, losing
his mom and dad. His uncle moving in here,
buncha ups and downs. Clint's been through it,
but you'd never even know it."

"Those two've been through it together," Skye adds.
"Clint's a good guy. Think he might like you too."

I look up at them both. Realize I have cold chills
covering my arms and it's still ninety degrees outside.
Think maybe it's time for me to reinvent myself.
Take a risk. Say yes to something unexpected.
Figure out ways to glow all on my own.

They both start to walk away
and then Skye looks back.
Right at me.

"Look, if you were serious about helping us,
working with us or whatever,

then let's do something about it.
Let's make music together."

Loving Me

What would it look like
if I just worked on forgiveness?
What if I held on to myself as tenderly
as possible? What if I just worked on grace
and showed myself as much love as I could?

Who would I be then?
What would that look like?
My god, I would love to try.

Job Applications

I spend the following morning
and every day that week downtown.

My whole past life gone in a second.
Disappeared. Lost to me.

We take turns with the car. Mom
drops me downtown. Goes to Dad.

My parents are no longer the ones
who can protect me. Care for me.

Keep me out of harm's way. My own
way. That's what I have to do now.

I go to every location I can walk
or take the bus to, but they're all full.

Every spot has already hired for summer.
I am too late for everything.

I don't get one place to call me back.
No one wants to get to know me more.

Deflated. Defeated. Three weeks into
summer and my life feels lost to me.

Coming Clean

A week later,
I pull up to the complex
and Clint is sitting outside our door.
His legs sprawled out in the sunshine.
His face tilted toward the sky.

"I was waiting for you," he announces.
"Wanted to hear your news.
Any job offers? What do you got?"

And he is so earnest. Wants to know
so bad, that it breaks me all the way down.

And I stand there in the middle
of the hottest summer on record.
Southern heat. Climate change.
End of the world kind of steamy.
And I just start to cry. Something
I have done so little of since it happened.
Since we were served and Dad left
and stayed gone. I cry so much
and so hard, I start to choke and cough.

Clint rushes over, grabs his water bottle,
and tells me to sit. Makes me drink.
Puts his hand on my shoulder
and just holds it there steady. Calm.

"Just breathe. It's okay. Sit. Breathe."

"I'm rich"

I say. As if it's a surprise. As if
this is some new idea or theory.

"Okay," Clint says.

"No, you don't understand.
Rich like ridiculous,
stupid amounts of money.
I'm Chloe Brooks . . . of the infamous
Brooks family . . . I am . . .

"Yeah, I know," he says,
cuts me off and looks at me
like we're just meeting.

"What?"

"We all know. I mean . . . we read
the news. I've seen the papers.
I know who you are. Chloe Brooks
of Clark and Lana Brooks.
Brooks Associated," he says,
looking dead at me.
"We all know who you are,"
he says again.

I say nothing in response.
Just shut my mouth.
Because I realize
he also knows

that we are not rich
anymore.

"So you all were just
humoring me? Just making fun
of me? Pretending you didn't know?"

"We didn't pretend anything.
You never offered it up. Fact is
you haven't hardly said a word about yourself
since you got here. A little stuck-up
is all I thought. Was just waiting
for you to share. But it's not . . .
a surprise."

"I got a secret too"

Clint says. "We know each other."

"What? What do you mean?
No, we don't."

"We do. We've definitely met.
James and Skye too."

"Uhh . . . no way. I would totally
remember meeting you all. Come on.
Stop playing." I stare back at Clint.
He is unmoved.

"The three of us sometimes cater.
Usually around Derby season
they need a buncha teenagers
to come and serve fancy hot dogs
wrapped in dough or whatever.
They been hiring us since we turned sixteen.
We know you. Fact is, we worked
every single party y'all had last summer.
And seriously, you had soo many parties."

"Oh my god, I do remember you," I flush.

It comes rushing back to me. My face
goes red hot. I remember Lily and Declan,
all of us ordering everyone around.
Remember us making fun of Clint
behind his back. Talking about how country,
how skinny, how awkward, how tall,

how anything that was outta place.
We couldn't get enough.
It comes rushing back to me.

How we kept asking all three of them
to say certain words certain ways
as if we all weren't from Kentucky.

Oh. My. God.

Shame

rushes over me,
floods me full
of regret and fear.
Feel like falling,
stumbling,
tripping,
crashing
in on myself,
can't see
the way,
don't want
to see
myself
anymore.

My apology

feels false,
tired,
wimpy,
feels
rushed,
feels
weak,
winded,
winding
all the way down.

This *I'm Sorry*
is shaky,
crumbling,
not
enough.

But I say it anyway.

And somehow

Clint accepts it.

Spoiler Alert

"I am also unhireable.
I am a total jerk
who treated you like crap
and even now you're still
helping me, but no one
will hire me.
As in what is a job?
Everything is all filled up.
I missed the whole hiring process.
And I spent the whole week
downtown, wasting my time
and trying to get people,
anyone really, to see me
or want to get to know me
or want to spend time
getting to know me.
I am completely
and totally
useless."

"I wanna get to know you,"
Clint says and smiles.
All those teeth.
All that laid back,
all that confidence.

I don't know why he is still
talking to me or why
he still cares,
but somehow
he does.

Stop Being Scared

"You can't hide that fact that you really don't
wanna be here. It's like you're afraid of us,
of this life, or this apartment building."

"I am. I mean . . . I was. I'm not gonna lie,
I was told my whole teenage life
that I wasn't supposed to come to this part
of town. Told that this city is divided
and once you cross over,
you get into a dangerous part.
Where you could get robbed or shot
or raped or killed. Those are actual things
that people said to me. My family, my friends.
As if this whole part of the city was off-limits.
It was. I never came over here. It's just . . .
the way I was brought up. So now I'm here.
In the place I was told wasn't safe.
And everyone was wrong, by the way.
I just fell for it. Just fell for this idea of a place
that could hurt you. A place to stay away from."

"And how do you feel now?" Clint asks,
looking like he genuinely needs to know.
Looking like he has so many more questions.
Looking like he could stay here all day.

"Now I feel like such a loser.
I just listened to everything people told me.
Was perfectly fine to think of the city divided.
This half is safe. This half is dangerous.
And if you live in one part of the world

you can't cross over into the other.
So I played into that. Kept that story going.
And I feel so ignorant.
Like I could have stopped it or questioned it
or pushed back against it. And now I'm here.
And everything they said was a lie.
Now I know the truth."

"So what are you gonna do about it?"

Clint asks. Staring straight into my eyes.

"How you gonna change it?
The way they see us?
The way they see you?"

The questions hang there,
look me right in the face.

The Truth

I see Natalia that night in the laundry room.
She gives me a knowing nod when I start
to separate everything like she told me.

"I'm sorry," I say finally. "For not listening,
for not paying attention. I . . . I'm sorry."
I say it out loud, even though my words
don't feel sufficient or enough.
They sound hollow coming out of my mouth.
Natalia knows it. We both do.

"You don't have to be sorry, Chloe.
This whole . . . this whole apology
just feels like an act to me.
And I gotta be honest.
I kinda don't believe it."

I don't blame her, but I push on.
"I know. I feel like I was just caught up
in my past. And it was fake. It wasn't real.
It was this imaginary place of safety and beauty.
I was looking at one thing and the reality
was something totally and completely different.
That's what I can't stop thinking about.
I want to be someone different too.
I want to be my realest self.
The one I can actually be proud of.
You know? I just don't want to be . . ."

Poor

"You don't want to be what?" Natalia asks,
looking at me clear now. Like she's finally
seeing me for the first time.
"Poor? Is that what you think?
Is that how you see me—how you see all of us?"

"It's not that. That's not what I mean.
I don't think of you in that way . . . I don't . . ."
And then I stop. Stop making things up as I go.
Stop lying to everyone and especially to myself.
Stop trying to prove I'm something that I'm not.
Stop all the make believe.

"You're right. I don't wanna be poor," I say,
and shame finds a way of sneaking up beside me,
stares right at me as if I've committed the one sin
I can't take back. I know it's wrong, but I can't unfeel it.

"Well, finally. The truth," Natalia says,
and I can see her see me completely
for the first time.

Not Me Anymore

"Just because I miss some of the stuff from my old life
doesn't mean I miss who I was back then.
I like this person a whole lot more,
or at least . . . I'm trying to."

"You got this." Natalia says, sitting on top of the dryer.
"And I hear you and I get it. I know it's not been easy.
Heard you couldn't find a job either."

I join her on the dryer.
"Nope. I spent all last week trying to get one,
and guess what? No one's hiring anymore.
They're definitely not hiring me."

"Chloe, look. We all know your summer
isn't what it was supposed to be. Oh well.
But I gotta tell you the truth.
You got two choices.
You can sit around
and be all sad for yourself
or you can get off your ass
and do something," Natalia says.

I start to laugh—can't even help myself.

"No, you're right. I know, I know.
But I have no idea what to do."

"Well, if you can't figure out what to do
for yourself, then figure out something to do
for somebody else. You ever thought of that?"

Our Old Kentucky Home

Spotless
Immaculate
Graceful
Bright
Elegant
Sparkling
Flawless
Pure

Our New Kentucky Home

Disheveled
Sloppy
Disarrayed
Unkempt
Dilapidated
Messy
Dirty
Neglected

That's the word
I stay stuck onto.
"Neglected."
Because it's us,
my family,
that did
all the damage.
We are the ones
responsible.
We are the ones
at fault here.

"Neglected."
Yes,
that's the word.

Kentucky—Take One

There are two states of Kentucky.
I know that now. The one I was born into,
all horse money and bourbon,
all stately hotels built in the 1920s
that serve mint juleps and old-fashioneds
with cherries and syrup. The old-school. Old style.
The born into money. The you can't touch me
or anything I own. The always wanting more.
The Kentucky that has the Derby,
the old Run for the Roses. Horse farms
and white picket fences. The Kentucky
that has the distilleries and the breweries.
The one that makes money on itself.
That's the one I am used to.
Private schools and walled off from everything.
Lexington is horse country for sure.
And my family played all the parts in that.
Owned the sprawling mansion, had all the help,
owned hotels downtown and a horse farm.
Had all the everything that money could buy
and then even more than that.
Went to all the parties, had all the glitz and glamour
you could ever want. We have always been accustomed
to more and more.

Kentucky—Take Two

And now I am here.
On the outside of town
in Limestone and a part of the city
that my father always told me was not safe.
It was good enough for other people,
but not for us. Never for us.
I was born into a world of protection
and save you from everything.
Born into a world of gated communities
and alarm systems and you can never be too safe.
Born to be protected and kept away
from the rest of the world—the one they said
could scare or harm or hurt you.
I was raised in a cocoon.
And now I am fully out of it
and in the world on my own.

This Kentucky is so different
from the one I was born into.
I am ashamed that I never realized
there was more than what I was raised up with.
Who did I think I really was after all?

People have ideas, stereotypes,
misconceptions about this side of town,
the one I was kept away from,
the one my mom grew up in,
the one I am suddenly
trying desperately
to be a part of.

BUILDING BACK UP

An Invitation

"We have to make this right,"
Mom says when I tell her
that they've all been to our house,
and that they spent last summer
serving us. She aims to fix it
and invites everyone over for lemonade.

We fix up the apartment best we can.
She mixes iced tea into the lemonade
and Clint, Skye, James, and Natalia
all sit squeezed on the couch
or around the card table.

"I cannot believe you all worked
as caterers at our home
and we did not know.
I am so embarrassed," she says,
gesturing at Clint, Skye, and James.
"We never expected this to happen.
But I am so, so happy that you all
are in Chloe's life, because this summer
has been hard, really hard."

I cringe so hard I might pass out.

"Did Chloe tell you all I grew up here?"

I had absolutely not told them this.
I grab her hand to try and get her
to stop talking. She does not
get the hint.

We Own This Apartment Complex

Clint almost chokes on his lemonade.
"I'm sorry, what did you say?
Your apartment complex?
What do you mean?"

"Oh, we own this place. Now.
We didn't when I was growing up.
My dad was the super here
and then finally worked long enough
to buy it when they put it up for sale.
When my parents passed away, it became
the beginning of all our businesses."

I am fully dying inside.

Skye, James, and Natalia all look at me.
What can I even say? What does it even
matter anymore?

"It's true"

I tell them, when I see everyone outside.
"We own it. And we've let it all go.
I am sorry for my family, for me.
I wanna do something.
For you all, for us."

Skye, James, and Natalia watch close.
Knowing my family has let everyone down.
They stay staring at me. Wondering. Judging?
I can't tell.

"I wanna do it for you all," I say.

"We're not charity," Natalia says.
'We don't need any of your handouts.
You should know that by now."

"Okay, fine, you're right.
I wanna do it for me.
I want to feel better, okay?!
You got me.
Let me do this."

"No one's stopping you.
Make it happen," James says.
Full of love.

"I love you all!" I call out,
repeating the line I've heard them say
to each other so many times.

Surprising both myself
and everyone who can hear me.

"We love you right back," Clint says,
so everyone can hear him too.

Later that night, after everyone else is asleep

I hear a small knock on my window.
Clint Jackson. At your service.

"Come outside," he whispers
when I pull the window open.
Can smell the Kentucky sky
in the air. All crisp and clean.
He helps me climb out
and we go sit in the field
together.

He says what I know he's been holding on to.
"I just . . . I can't believe y'all *own* this place."

He leans back and looks around
at the four buildings.

"And if that's really true, then why the hell
is it so run-down?" he asks,
pointing to the apartments,
that all look like they're starting to fall apart.

The term "slumlord," pops up in my mind
and I can't get it out.
It's true. The paint starting to peel,
the jam of the screen doors,
the locks that don't work.
And I know we're in one of the nicer apartments,
so what do the other ones look like?

"Never mind, I know why . . ."

This is how Clint starts,
and once he starts,
he doesn't stop.

"There is a disregard for poor people.
You know that, right?
As if we're the ones who've made all the mistakes.
We're the ones who've messed it all up for ourselves.
Dug our own graves and all of that.
I know I'm poor. I know there was a certain way
you looked at me and all of us when you first got here.
I know we been late on the rent before
and I know this place hasn't been taken care of
for a long stretch. I know we're from the same state
but are worlds apart. I know that.
Can see it with my own eyes.
Doesn't make it any easier or better.
Fact is, I want to rage against a system that's set up
for me to fail. You know, my uncle gets sick
and he doesn't get paid. There's not paid time off for him.
And there's no big ole net surrounding us
that's supposed to take care of us or hold us.
That doesn't exist for everyone.
Fact is, it exists only for a few people."

I know Clint is right.
Lately, I have been thinking he is right
about everything that I was so sure about.
All the maybes and ifs that I grew up with,
he is right on about.

"Stuck here"

He keeps on . . .

"It's like this constant balancing act
that we stay playing. Every single day.
At the grocery store, for all of our bills,
out in the world. Like we're always
navigating and negotiating
what it takes to survive.
This is no extra and no savings.
Life feels like an avalanche
and I'm spending all this time counting
and running, running, and counting.
Seeing if I can make it out alive
and if Skye and James and Natalia
can come on with me.
Seeing if we can run fast enough together
or who will be left behind? That's toxic.
That weighs you down.
And if all you ever see
is the same kind of sadness
kicked up all around you,
then you start to get down too,
and I have trouble getting out of my head
and just letting it all go.
I can't let anything go."

Silence

I do not answer.
Don't think he's waiting on me to,
but I stay quiet just the same.
I turn myself down.
Know that he doesn't need me on ten,
doesn't need all the extra
that is running around in my head.
I go quiet and decide that listening
will make this better,
even if it won't make it go away.

"There is the kind of poor you are
when you feel like you're middle class
but you've got more than other people,
and then there's the kind of poor you are
when you have no money left over
at the end of the month
after you've maybe paid all the bills.
That's the kind of poor we are.
But everything changed
When my mom and dad died.
I realized without the people
I loved most in the whole world,
that money didn't matter to me.
I knew I needed it, but I also knew
it wasn't gonna define me
and I wasn't gonna let other people
look down on me because of something
that wasn't even my fault. I let go.
I had Skye and James coming over
every single day. Nonstop.

Some of the time, we'd just sit there.
Silence. Not watching something,
or checking something, or looking
at our phones or computers. Just being.
Just sitting. I had to learn to like myself
again. And remember how Mom and Dad
made me feel. So in all that quiet, we just
listened to this," he says, holds his hand out
to the sky, the grass, the setting sun. The land.

We Stay Silent Together

Clean smell of Kentucky. Air thick
and heavy on our skin. Slick with sweat.
I try my hardest not to let Clint hear me
breathe. Because I can't catch all that breath.
All that extra. All those fireflies in my chest.
Grass thick beneath me. Ants and beetles
crawling beside me. Mud below. "Be one,"
Clint whispers. And I want to laugh,
but it's that same nervousness, same
tickle inside of me. Don't reach for his hand
so when his is suddenly on top of mine,
I inhale so hard he can hear me for sure.
So presses on my palm. I stay here.
In this moment. The in and out. The let go,
the extra second it takes to not be perfect
or right or better than anyone else. To just
be us. Right now. Nowhere else but here.

Together.

"We are broke"

I finally say it. Plain and fast
so that I don't have to explain myself,
but know full well I am going to need to.

"Like really broke,
or like you're just hanging here for a spell?"

I love the way he talks.
Country and right here
and a little off. I love
the sound of his voice
and want to keep on hearing it.

"No, like really broke. Like the news is right on.
Like our house was put into foreclosure,
whatever the hell that means. It's gone.
We have nothing."

Clint starts to laugh now
and smiles in my direction.
"This hasn't been easy on you has it?
For real."

"I don't even know who I am
without all my stuff. Without all the extra
that I used to think made me who I was,
who I am. I miss it. I miss shopping.
I miss buying . . . anything, everything.
I miss the way spending money made me feel.
It made me feel so powerful. And pretty.
And like I could do and say anything.

Could make anything happen.
That's what money does to a person.
It changes you. And so living without it
changes you too. Makes you feel empty in a way,
not good enough. Sort of lost.
I haven't really said that out loud until now.
And I think I gotta change this feeling."

Mom Is Cooking and I Get Called Home

"Chloe, honey, can you help with this?"

And I can. Pull out the garlic and onions,
the scallions and catfish. Start slicing.

"I have some news I want to share with you."

I look up at her. Can't wait any longer.
I need to know the truth.

"Mom, why did you and Dad let this place fall apart?"

"That's what I want to talk to you about.
Look, we made a mistake. We just got so busy
with other businesses and it became something
we couldn't manage anymore, so we outsourced.
We hired an agency and trusted they were doing
all the repairs, but we never checked in on it,
we never did our job as owners,
we just let it all deteriorate,
let it all crumble basically.
We had so many other things
to think about and to do,
that this place fell through,
just became forgotten.
But I want you to know
I went back to the lawyer
and we are taking control now.
It is fully in our possession
and I am taking over as the super."

"The super what?!"

"The superintendent of the building.
Just like Papaw. Let me introduce myself.
My name is Lana Jones Brooks.
How may I help you?"

"Are you kidding me? You? The super?"

"Don't act so surprised. You know my superpowers
are coming back to me every single day,"
she says, the pan starting to sizzle and smell
sweet and glorious. Fish and grits.
A meal we never had before we moved
to Limestone. I am starting to see her
in a whole new way.

"And I have some other news too.
I spoke to the director of the camp
and with the extra money coming in,
we could spend a little of that to send you.
Salvage some of your summer after all.
You'd leave this week. Surprise!"

I pause. Can see the Los Angeles skyline.
Can see the new friends, the music lessons.
Can hear my voice getting stronger, louder.
But when I look at that future, it's not a me
I recognize anymore.

Mom interrupts my thoughts.
"Just think about it.

Now slice some of those tomatoes.
I got them from the farmers' market.
They taste just like the land."

That Night

I knock on Clint's window
and ask him to come outside.

He opens it up and looks dead at me.
"Go home, Chloe."

"What? Why? Come out here!"

"Look, I don't have time for this.
I didn't want to, but I heard your mom.
Heard you're leaving this week, heard summer camp
is back on. Congratulations!
So . . . what else do you want me to say?"

"You were listening to our conversation?"

"I think you forget that this place is run-down
and you can hear everything. All of it.
And I was sitting at the picnic tables . . . But
that's not even what this is about.
You were never gonna stay here anyway.
This isn't you, right?
You got bigger plans, better things to do.
You can't be part of this ugly, small, shitty place.
You don't have time for this or even for us,"
he finishes and starts to move inside.

I put my hand on the window. "I'm staying,"
I say. "You didn't hear all of it. You don't know
the whole story. I'm not going anywhere."

He Crawls Outside

His body is magnetic. Can see him maneuver
and shape-shift so we're standing under the stars
together, and he picks me up, up, up off the ground
and his mouth is on mine finally. Shimmering.
Glowing and on me. And breathing beside me.
And then we are up against the wall and the rain
that was threatening to come down earlier today
is now pouring. Over us, on top of us. I hold his face
in the palms of my hands, close my eyes and feel
my body start to firecracker beside him. Heat,
wet, the smell of the sky opening up above us.

"I'm not going anywhere," I whisper to him.
"Not this summer. Not ever."

The Next Morning

I sit outside our apartment
with Mom. The two of us
no longer just linked by loss.
Admit that I'm at fault too.
Something I have not wanted
to hold on to, something
I was trying to get away from.
The fact I never questioned
all the excess. The truth
that I always wanted more,
was always hungry for extra.
The fact I was always game
to make fun of people
who weren't like me,
didn't have it as good as me.
The truth I never learned
to do anything for myself.
Yes, I am at fault too.
And ready to change
that same old story.
Tell her I don't want to leave
and that I'm not going anywhere.

Do Something

Mom and I both
know the truth.
That doing nothing
got us into
this situation.
That doing nothing
left us
with nothing,
believing in
nothing,
with nothing
at all to do.

And I am tired
of it. Exhausted.
Worn out
of doing
nothing.

So it's time
for us to do
something.

Make it right
somehow,
some
way.

We Call Dad

Want to tell him our plan
to fix up the apartments,
to make it right, better.

He is in his own head,
spinning around us,
vibrating with thoughts.

Keeps saying this:

"Wealth is war."

He saw it on a commercial
for some show about millionaires or billionaires
so he keeps on saying it on the phone.
How he'll fight for our life back.
Wants us back.
All of our possessions too.
Wants to get out of jail.
Wants to prove his innocence,
show how he was wronged.
Doesn't want to take the blame.
Keeps blaming everyone else.
How money can incite
violence. Brutality.
Jealousy. Trauma.
Pain. Tells us he is hurting.

How much he is willing to fight
for us, for our life,
for him.

We get off the phone,
both of us
in tears.

Reframe

I tell Mom we have to find
another way to exist.
That having more
is not the only way.
Fact is, it's no way
at all. Just extra.
Just stuff.

In bed, I write this.
I mean it, I start
to dream it.
Write it down.

Wealth is the sunshine
arching high atop the trees.
Sky reaching, rounding, frolicking.
It is the winding hilltops.
The way Clint's palm
feels on my lower back,
hip, waist. Shake.
My head a jumble
of what everything is worth.

Wealth is love.
Is falling in love.
And figuring out
how to last, withstand,
make it through the night
and look forward to the morning.

Make It Right

This place can't be forgotten
anymore. I wake up ready
to do something. Anything
that doesn't involve
sitting around all day
feeling sorry for myself.

"This is our place," I announce
to Mom who is clearly
on her third cup of coffee
and ready to roll.

"It sure is. And you and me
are gonna make Papaw
proud as hell."

"Yes!" I shout, not caring
who hears me or who's listening.
"And we can use all the money from rents
to fix it up then? To put it back into
the apartments? Into the complex?"

We smile. In it together.

"And I want to grow a garden
and treat this place like we own it
once and for all. Because we do," Mom says.

"I have a plan too. I've got two hands,
you've got two hands, right?
Let's walk around and see what needs

the most attention. First,
let's fix up the rickety old picnic table
and the junky swing set
and plant something that blooms,
instead of weeds growing up
all over the place.
Make it something beautiful
not something to always
get away from.
Make it home."

"Let's do it"

Mom's voice sings beside mine.
Knowing she is in it with me.
Here for it too.

"But first, we need some good country food.
It's time you started loving my side of Kentucky.
Not just the fancy. Not just the manicured
or perfect. Not just the parties or the benefits
or the kind of Kentucky you're used to.
It's time you started learning your history.
Learning you."

I hug her tight around the waist. Hold on.

"We're riding to Indy's for fried chicken."

"Mom, I've had fried chicken before."

"Yeah, but never at Indy's."

We Drive Around

Before we eat, Mom cruises.
Her directions this time. Her pace.
Through the cornfields, winding hills,
and back roads first. Points out
what she loves. Directs me to roll
the windows all the way down,
smell that sweet Kentucky air.
Says she grew up running outside
in all seasons to get a sense of home.
Said her dad knew the best hollers
and the best creek beds, mud holes,
spots to disappear. Said maybe it's time
I did some disappearing too. Quiet
my mind. Learn my history. Hers
and her family's. Study the music,
the photographs, the language
of the Bluegrass. Banjos and clogs,
corn bread and sour mash. Discover
who I come from and who I really am.

Mom Orders

It is as if we have not eaten
for days, and it feels that way to me.
Hunger in a way I haven't felt in so long.
Fried okra, onion rings,
and corn on the cob.
Pecan pie and spicy wings.
So we eat. Apple cobbler too.
Sitting in a shiny booth inside.
The city feels all alive and alight.
I feel both city and country somehow.
Can't even tell where this state begins
and I end. Feel a whole new sense of self.
What we need to do to make it right.

Mom Tells Me What She Does Not Miss

"I do not miss
keeping up with
everyone.
Everything new,
everything bought
and shared
and posted about.
I do not miss feeling
like I wasn't enough
even when I had
everything.
I do not miss
the keeping up with,
the endless search
for more.
The bigger vacations,
the better stories,
the more clothes,
the better service,
the all the time
trying
to prove something
or prove my worth
or more than that,
to prove my worth
to other people.

I do not miss that
at all."

"This is home"

Mom says on the drive home. Swirl of traffic,
half dozen convenience stores, two liquor stores,
handful of check cashing spots, and Indy's,
which was just as delicious as Mom promised.

"Kentucky is complicated. It's a whole universe
I can't always understand. Or get my head around.
I'm trying hard to love my roots. Trying to stay
here but all I wanna do sometimes is get back
to our old life. The one that left us behind.
But I know there is no going back now."

When she says this, I look up. See her new again.
Know it has been just as hard for her too.
Reframe. Reimagine. Make new again.
We need to start over. Reintroduce ourselves.

"You're not alone, you know? You got me.
We can do this together."

Ways My Mom Has Changed

"Chloe, I am finished
with outsourcing my whole entire life.
I am done with it.
I let someone else raise you
and let someone else clean our home
and run our calendars
and drive us around
and cook for us
and take care of us in every single way.
Now I am taking control of my life again
and taking control of yours too.
I want to be the one who makes the calls
and who makes dinner.
I haven't cooked in so many years.
I am still trying to figure out who I am
without your father and all of his ideas
about how we were supposed to live.
He wanted us all to fit in a certain box,
to fit in the frame of his life
and how he wanted us to be framed.
I am over that now.
No, not over it, but I am fighting against it.
No longer tied up with those ideas, or ideals,
and I don't want that for you either.
I want you to try new things
and live a life that is not so tied up in money.
We just got caught up
in the business and trying to always make more.
There is such a thing as too much.
I know your father didn't always see that.
I still don't think that is clear for him,

but it's true. We had too much,
and now we have nothing.
So I want to build it up from here.
I want to figure out who we are at the bottom.
Bare bones.
Who are we without all that extra
hanging around?
And I want you to find that out too."

And So I Do

Work at discovering myself.
Can feel my whole body unwind.
Become untethered to the past.
To who I was and what I wanted.
To the kind of life
I thought I needed
to live.

Shut down social media.
Learn what is left
now that we don't own
a damn thing.

Who are we now?
With nothing
to hang on to?
Sitting on land
that doesn't even belong
to us and never actually did.
Reckoning.
Rude awakening.
Uproar.

So we sit outside.
In the same silence
Clint told me about.
Listen. Take it in.
Know we can work.
Know we can face it.
Know it will be hard,
but know what needs
to be done.

At Night

I lie awake.
Think about my role here
and what I need to do
to make it all right.

Decide that this is the summer
I let it all go.
The one that lets it all loose.
The one where I survive.
Take all of me apart.
The one where I peel back
the layers of who I used to be.
The summer we go on and firework.
Break on open heartbreak.
Bust it loose. Show off.
This is the summer I do not
lose hold of who I am
and who I am supposed to be.
The summer Mom finds
herself and us again. The one
where Dad starts to tell
the truth. For real this time.
And we become the versions
of ourselves that we can be proud of.

The Week Flies By

Mom makes breakfast every morning
and starts to teach me how. Biscuits.

Homemade everything. Fried eggs,
hash brown casseroles, grits, and gravy.

She is remembering her past, who she
used to be. It's not as far as she thought.

We take notes around the place
and jot down all that needs to be done.

It feels never-ending. All I do is work
until everyone gets home. My hands raw.

Seeing Clint becomes the shining
part of my day. Want to talk and impress.

Want to show off and be near him.
Never met anyone like him. Trust

that I want to be better. Know more,
do more. Make it all happen.

I feel changed. So does my mom.
Every day. Most of all. We rally.

Things We Learn to Do

Make a budget.
Spruce up the space.
Do the laundry.
Empty the machines.
Wipe the counters.
Wash the floors.
Clean behind everything.
Tighten the swing set.
Paint the swing set.
Paint the shutters.
Paint the apartment doors.
Paint everything that is chipping,
everything that is fading.
Finish the picnic table.
Sand the wood.
Weed the garden.
Mow the lawn.
Plant new flowers.
Plant new life.
Fix the trash bins.
Fix the recycling bins.
Take out the trash.
Bring it back in.
Mark the recycling.
Start the composting.
Replace the light bulbs.
Replace the fencing.
Repaint the fence,
every time we mess up,
do it all again.

Replace the letters
on the sign.

"Limestone Apartments."

See it shine.

Clear My Mind

Keep working, keep my head down,
keep my focus still, still fixing, still
trying to make it all right. Sweating,
struggling, mending, still breaking.

"You need to rest," Clint says,
coming up to sit beside me in the dirt.

"I have to fix this. I have to finish.
There's too much work to do. I can't."

"You can. You gotta. Also, the swing set
looks soooo good! That new paint job!
Even the swings aren't squeaking.
Just sit with me already."

And so I do. And before I know it,
I'm pumping my legs up and down
and throwing my head back
into the great big sky above me.
I can smell Kentucky all over me.
Smells of hills and mud, dirt
and forgiveness or something close
to that. I will forever be trying
to figure out what I mean here
or how we landed here. All of it
stays steady and lodged inside my head.

"Just let it all go," Clint calls out,
and he's swinging so high and so fast
that I start to believe him

and I do.

I fly.

He Jumps into the Sky

And so do I. Our bodies
reaching and then tumbling.
Fumbling over each other,
tossing and falling. My heart
stretching and aching. Arms
holding, hands touching.
To be this close is to feel
breathless. Wasted with want,
suddenly about to get just
what I have been dreaming of.
The way his skin smells like hay
and the fields out back. Seeing
how maybe he finally sees me
the way I want to be seen.
So I take a risk, roll on top
of him, can smell the clean
cut bluegrass on our skin.
Intoxicated by his smile,
and I lean into him, his lips
finding mine. Steady, needing,
craving this touch. This hunger.
We kiss like this, air thick
and steady around us, until
the sun begins to make the sky
golden behind us. Delirious.
Can't get enough of this.
Want to stay right here,
loving this moment, him,
this state, this night, this heat,
but most of all myself. So much
more than I ever have before.

Close My Eyes

My head on his shoulder
in the cool of the grass.
The dirt on the ground
marking us.

I want to stay this way,
curled beside him, his
long arms loose around me.

"I wrote something,"
he says finally, his breath
tickling my neck.

"A song?" I ask.

"I don't know yet. A poem,
the beginning of a story.
Just something I've been
thinking of."

"Read to me. Will you?"

He pulls out a small notebook.
One I've seen him carry around,
but never heard him share from.

What I Carry with Me

The way Mama and Daddy
would call my name like a song
each morning. Their voices singing.
The coffee my papaw would drink
from a bowl to cool it off.
Mountains in the morning.
Tobacco growing high
into the sky. Bourbon cooking
in the air. My uncle's pickup truck.
Quitting smoking. Not being
who they think I am. Pushing
past expectations. My boundaries
lasting. Living longer
than they think I will.
Living at all. Want to last
as long as I can. Here.
With you.

I Kiss Him Longer

Steadier.
Harder.
Deeper.

"More," I say.
"I want to hear you read
or sing. Forever. I love it."

He smiles, shakes his head no,
rubs his hands over his face.
Embarrassed. Nervous.

"Don't do that. You have to take
a compliment," I say. Realizing
that maybe I can teach him
something too. "Own it.
You wrote that. You can sing.
You can play. You are the best,
the kindest person I have ever,
ever met. You say I love you
to everyone, and also
to the flowers
and the sky
and the clouds,
and you smile
first thing in the morning.
How do you do it?!
You just stay open
and so vulnerable
and easy to love."

He tilts his head, grins bigger.

"You are. You have to know it.
You have to embrace that thing.
That superstar, golden boy,
shining sun thing you've got.
Write all the poems and songs.
Do all the gigs, record, play!
Just don't keep it all to yourself.
That'd be selfish and you're not—"

He kisses me back

to stop me from talking.

"It's too much," he says,
between his lips on mine.
"But I hear you, I do.
I been reading all these poets
that Skye has been bringing me
from the library. And I'm into it."

I look at him. Love the way his mind
spins and works. Somersaults all over.

"You ever heard of Crystal Wilkinson?
Ross Gay? Wendell Berry?
Aimee Nezhukumatathil? I mean
they are writing about the land
and love and home. I just . . . I want
to be like that. Write like that.
Sing like that."

"Well, then you gotta share it too,"
I say. He nods before leaning into me
again and kissing my neck this time.
The sky going dark. But my heart
lighting all the way up.

Go to Sleep

seeing

    floating

        dreaming

    flying

imagining

    drifting

        gliding

    waving

swooping

    soaring

        fantasizing

    visioning

swimming

    sailing

        loose

    live

free

All of Me Feels Renewed

I finally understand
what needs to be done.
Concentrate on the feeling,
the moment, what I am trying
to make happen. My hands
covered in Kentucky soil,
the dirt underneath fingernails.
I erase my past. Keep digging.
Shake away who I used to be
and who people knew me as.
Take that away. Get to know
what I want. The things I need
to make it all worth living.
Something blooming. Life
to take care of. Community
surrounding me that loves
who I am, not what I'm worth.
Worthy of love. Of time spent.
Of goodness and beauty.
Of clarity and hope.
Of calm and surrender.
Of just being
me.

Every Day

We spend outside. Me and Mom.
Getting the yard cleaned up.

Getting my mind cleared out.
Sweep. Dig. Plant. Paint.

Repeat. Repeat. Repeat.
Get in a meditation.

Count backward. Take stock.
Believe I can make it better.

Change the shape
of who I am

and where I come from.

Text Lily

You cooled off yet?
Can we start again?
I miss you.
Catch me up?

Lily texts

Been thinking of you too.
Miss you too.
Where are you?

Text Lily

Limestone Apartments
Other side of town.
Come visit?

Lily texts

I overreacted. I know.
I'm sorry too.
Tell me where and when
I'll be there.

Staying In It

I let myself take a risk. Might get hurt
but I want to take the chance. Miss
my friends. Lily mostly and want her to see
who I have become, how I have changed.
I let the air wash over me in a way.
It's still hot enough to only wear shorts
and T-shirts, but I can start to feel the coolness
and can imagine this place in the fall and winter.
It's true. I do not want to go back to my old life
and the way things used to be. Just to feel this way.
Just to feel a kind of nothing. Wash over me too.

Take my phone out and put my AirPods in.
Let music take me another way, let it lead me.
My mind gets clear, gets opened all the way up.

Think of all the things Clint has said to me,
all the ways he has opened up this state to me,
all the ways he has opened up his heart to me.

Every day, I get closer to Clint too—

"Come on. You been working so hard
out here. Let me cook something for you."

"You cook?" I ask and cannot hide my smile.
"You for real cook?"

"Yeah, you know I do. I for real cook. Real food."

"And it's good as hell," Skye says.

"So you make corn bread?"

"Uhhh . . . among other things, yeah, I do.
I make corn bread. And fried green tomatoes
and fried chicken and fish and grits
and chicken-fried steak and corn pudding
and what do you want? I got it. I can make it."

"Who taught you?" I ask, wanting to know.
Thankful my mom is finally teaching me.

"My dad. He did all the cooking.
And he said if I was worth anything in life,
I had to learn how to work the grill, the stove,
the oven. Had to be someone who could cook up
something that would fill us up.
That's all I'm aiming to do. You know?"

"Well, then let's get cooking," Skye says
and looks my way.

How to Make Corn Bread
According to Clint

"First we need the ingredients.
Cornmeal. We use Weisenberger plain.
It's local. Over Midway. And it's good.
Oil or bacon grease. Baking powder,
baking soda, salt, eggs, and buttermilk."

"Bacon grease?"

"Or oil. Yeah, you heard right.
You don't have to act so surprised."

Clint moves around the kitchen
all comfortable and slow.
Patient with everything he does.
Deliberate. I love watching the way
he works. The way he does everything
so skilled, so calm.

"You're gonna help, right?
Not just stand there and watch me."

And I realize that's what I have been doing.
Watching. Studying. Seeing what he will do.
What will happen next. Waiting. Wanting.

"Go 'head and preheat the oven to four hundred degrees.
And pour some of that bacon grease on the skillet.
About two tablespoons," he says,
acting like I can eyeball it.

"I need help"

"Already?" He takes the cast-iron skillet from me
and pours the grease on it.
It's been sitting on his counter.
"Takes about five minutes or so."

Now it's time to get mixing, so we do.
All the ingredients swirling in the bowl.
We whisk and mix, stir and fold.

"But don't stir too much.
You gotta let it breathe,
gotta let it sit out a little on its own.
You know?"

I do not know.
Once again realizing
that I am still learning.

While we wait,
Clint plays music.

Carolina Chocolate Drops

The sound is haunting.
The voices. The rhythm.
And the banjo starts.
And the lyrics roll.

And these new friends
who feel like family
are everywhere around me
clapping and singing about corn bread
and butter beans and making love.
And I think, *Oh! I want this too.* What is real.
What is true. *Yes, my god. I want this too.*

Clint sings in my ear. His voice low and clear.
Steady beside me. A rumble. A hum. A flow.

"You've been trying to get out so bad
maybe you missed everything
that's right here. Waiting for you."

Music = Love

It's the haunting,
the lilt and hum,
it's the foot stomping
jump run around,
it's the wait, the long
the longing drum.
The moan, the ache.
It's the coming back.
Been waiting for you.
It's the sun on your face.
Touch. It's the tell.
Each spell. The rock,
the root. It's the heat,
the wind. The lemon
drop. Move, it's the
groove. The heart,
the unstop. This
want. This home.

"What is this song?"

I ask, nodding and loving it.

"Corn bread and Butter Beans," James says.
"Carolina Chocolate Drops.
Basically our inspiration.
The kinda group we wanna be."

"This idea that you can share a meal
and love and good, good food
and making love. It's sexy and cool
and just laid-back. I love it," Clint adds.
"You know that kind of deep, long-lasting.
That kind of good, good love. You get it?"

"Hell yeah," I say suddenly. Surprised at myself,
at my willingness to say yes. At the word "yes."

Feel like I might start crying looking out
on all this country. On all these hills, on all
this forever that's surrounding me. Want to hold
deep onto it. Say forever and mean it. Can see
each roll of each moment we've been together.
I know I'm not going back to my original life,
the one I spent forever trying to keep hold of.
Everything can change. I know this now.
Know my old self has vanished.

Everyone Singing

Suddenly, Clint, Skye,
James, and Natalia start
singing and their voices
take over. So one song
stops and their song
begins. Skye is clogging
on the beat-up old floor.
Mom hears it and joins.
She is clogging too
and singing! At the tip
top of her range,
which is not super high
and it's sooo awkward
I have to start laughing.
Because I don't want
to cry it's so beautiful.
And clunky and exactly
what I did not want
to happen, but I do not
care about what people think
of me. I am not in the moment
to record the moment
or photograph the moment
and post it or get likes about it
or approval or love for it.
I don't want to be about
the image anymore. Over it,
done, and moving past it.
Just live it. Just be in it.
Let my heart and lungs

and guts guide me now.
Who do I follow?
My own path.
Map my own future.

A Concert

"Look, if y'all don't play for other people
and you keep all this magic to yourself,
then that's just plain selfish," I say.

I'm standing up in the kitchen,
full of cornmeal and grease, smelling
just like Clint after his shifts. Don't care
what I look or sound like. Time for truth.

"The apartments are just about cleaned up.
Let's use that bulletin board out there.
Host a concert. Just play a few songs.
Just play what you know. Just show up.
You wanted me to manage you, right?
Let's book our first gig."

They all look at me like I've lost it,
but they know I'm right,
know deep down how good they are,
how true they sound.

"Long as you'll sing with us," Skye says.

"You know it."

And I look around.

Family.

Everywhere.

Not Her Anymore

I don't want to be the girl
that everyone is trying to fix.

The one that messes up
and can't get anything right.

Mistake after mistake. Unruly
and up in everyone's way.

The one they talk about
when she's not around. Gossip.

Say they can't believe she exists
the way she does. Bubble. Shade.

Can't be the one they whisper
all up and down about. Naive. Ignorant.

I don't wanna be all left behind,
believe a story about myself.

One that isn't true. A lie.
Fable. Short story. Whole fiction.

Girl in trouble because
she doesn't know any better.

I can't be the I'm sorry girl
forever. The how can I fix it.

The oops, my bad. The apology
girl. The can you ever forgive me kind.

The one that doesn't learn better.
The one always crying whole tears.

The one everyone rolls their eyes at.
All flailing and weeping.

I can't be her anymore. And the truth is,
I think I'm already on the way.

We Play

Every night. Practice.
Rehearse. Over and over.
We sing, Skye dances.
James styles, Natalia directs,
our voices harmonize.
Braid together, form a tapestry.
A quilt. It covers me up, holds me.

Can't Keep Our Hands Off Each Other

Clint texts.
Meet me outside. Tonight.

I want to see him always.
This new. This energy.
This hunger, this yearning.

                                        Tell me where.
                                        I will be there.
                                        Anywhere.

The Stables,
he writes.

I close my eyes
and can smell him
from the last time,
can feel his arms
wrapped around me
and this night
and this need
that's closer
than anything
I've ever felt.
And this want
that needs to get met,
that needs some place to go,
space to land.
My heart galloping
in my chest.

Come to me,
he writes.

And all I want
is to go.

"I wrote this for you"

I tell Clint soon as I see him.
Want him to know how much
he has stayed on my mind.
Steady, steady.

I want to exist with you.
Right here beside you.
Somersault alongside you.
Be with you.
All day with you.
Forever with you.
Sunny day with you.
Cloudy weather with you.
All day with you.
Want to ride with you.
All night with you.
Catch flight with you.
Be all right with you.
Because I love you
and want to know you
and want to hold you
and want to depend on you
and want you to dream with me
and want you to dream of me
and can't keep my life from you
and want to see you
and be with you
and dream beside you
and ride, ride, ride with you.

Like Love

Maybe it is the way the setting sun
hits the side of Clint's face
and it looks like he's in the spotlight,
like everything is shining so clearly on him.
He leans back in the grass
and puts his hand out toward mine.
Asks me if I want to sit
and watch the sun sink
down low in front of us.

"Come on," he says.
"We might as well watch the day
slip away. Do you want to?
With me?"

His body beside mine feels
like it could outlast forever,
run me into existence.
I could exist forever here
with him, beside him,
my back against his chest,
the smell of his hair filling me
up with him. With this, with
a kind of country hallelujah.
Intertwined. Looped together.

Maybe I didn't even know myself
before this, the Kentucky sky bursting
around me. Maybe I hadn't ever bothered
to find out.

The New Me

And it's the way he asks me questions
and waits for me to answer.
The way he slows it down
and takes his steady, sweet time.
I am thinking of his voice and his patience
and the way I want to sit in the tall grass
all night long. If this is love, then I want it.
Want to know more about him
and his dreams too.
I used to feel so caught up in my own
that I couldn't see anything else,
but that has changed, shifted.

I want to hold him in my arms
and tell him that it will be okay,
that we will be okay.
It is the end of summer
and it feels like the last few weeks
have lasted forever,
and when I look in the mirror
I don't recognize myself anymore.
I had an idea of who I was
or who I was supposed to be
and now when I see myself
I see an entirely new me.

Love

"You know, Clint Jackson sounds exactly like the name of a country
music star, so . . . all you need is to get to Nashville,
get signed, get some actual clothes, you know . . ."

"I am sorry, what did you say?"

"Get to Nashville, get signed . . ."

"Nah, nah. That part about the clothes,
'cause last I checked, you *love* my cutoffs
and the smell of this shirt," he pulls me toward him.
"Like you can't get enough of this look."

I pull back and look directly at him and he's right.
I cannot get enough of him, of this moment,
and so finally I say what I've been holding inside.

"I love you," I say. "Feel like I have loved you
since you took me riding on your bike downtown
and acted all cool and like you didn't need
anything to just be who you are. You are just you.
Every second that I spend with you feels like a prize.
I want to be better when I'm with you. What is that?
I just become undone with you, like I'm unraveling
or melting or something. Like some kind of fireworks
are going off in my body. I don't . . . I've never felt
like this, like electric or like I'm coming apart,
but I don't even care. I just want you. With me,
beside me. On top of me," I finish, pulling him
and all of his energy and heat right into me.

"I love you too," he whispers back.
"But you already knew that."

The night goes quiet, like it always does out here.
He holds the back of my neck in the palm of his hand.
The heat rises right out of it. I can feel him holding on.
Warm and full of heat below. My heart is a kind of on fire
that I have never even known.

One Week Later

The yard is almost done.
Clint, Skye, James, Natalia,
all of them looking at the work.
Seeing the flowers finally bloom.

We take it all in together.
Mark this last weekend
as the one where we invite
the whole apartment to come out.

"It's time for the ultimate potluck,"
Natalia says. "Got the invites here,
and we posted at Goodwill too.
Might as well have a big party, huh?"

She is right. So we ask folks all over.
The library, Dairy Bar. I even text Lily.
Still want to make it right. Call it
an open house. Name ourselves hosts.
And post on the bulletin board.

Mom knows how to throw a party.
Maybe not on a budget, but she's trying
and it shows. Both of us working hard
and steady. Showing up, showing out.

Let this be the night we own up
to who we are. Take our history,
acknowledge who we come from,
share it with the whole community.

"This isn't the end—it's just the start"

Clint holds me around the waist while we look
out on the yard, on how clean and pristine it is.

"Look at all this," he says.

"Feels hard to believe. I started out doing this for me,
but something changed along the way. Shifted.
I thought I had it all back then. Everything.
But I didn't even know what that meant."

He doesn't interrupt me, so I keep on.

"I thought because my family was worth
so much, that made us better than,
more worthy than, anyone else.
Got lost inside my own value
being tied up in money.
Got lost inside my head,
inside my greed, inside my status,
inside my wish for more and more.
Truth is, it gave me a fake sense of myself.
Having more meant I was more lovable,
greater, stronger, worth more."

Clint looks at me. His eyes full of tears.
Mine too. Because I know what's real now.

"That was all a lie. Just a beautiful mess.
Not worth anything in the end."

"But don't you see how much this place is worth now?
Look at this goodness. You did this."

"We did this," I admit. Look right at Clint
and he smiles.

"Yeah, yeah you're right. *We* did this.
But you were right here with us."

The Night Arrives

Crowds of folks show up,
bringing all the country cooking
with them. Fried chicken in buckets,
fried whiting, Cajun-fried catfish doused
in hot sauce, BBQ ribs from someone's kitchen,
whole watermelons sliced straight through,
pitchers of sweet tea and strawberry lemonade,
coolers for beer and bottles of bourbon.
Potato salad, macaroni salad, corn bread,
butter beans, shelled peas, fried green tomatoes
and corn on the cob slathered in butter.

It's a feast. A potluck and no one goes hungry.
It's all about the relationships. The transformations,
not the transactions. So we welcome and we serve,
and we laugh, we cry out when someone else
joins us. The neighbors, the family members.
When Lily walks in, I don't rush over, but we wave,
somehow trying to figure out how to call each other in
while still leaving the past behind.

The sun is getting ready to set in the sky.
All of the bluegrass looks alive and on fire tonight.
Oranges and reds bursting. I feel choked up
and like I could cry at any second. I missed so much
while I was busy living my old life.
Missed slowing down, missed the feeling of this,
of being a kind of weightless and a kind of free.

Mom Introduces Herself

"Lana Jones Brooks. I'm the new super here,"
she tells Clint's uncle, who looks suspect
but smiles in her direction
and then over to us.

Skye and James introduce their mom and dad.
Natalia's abuela comes over to say hello
and embraces Mom in a hug
but only after sharing a massive list
of things that still need to be done,
taken care of. No one is getting
let off the hook here.

"Yes, yes. I am taking notes. I know,
I know it has not been kept in the best
repair, and I . . . am sorry. It was . . . my fault
and I, we . . ." She looks over to me.
"We are working to make it better.
I know it won't be easy, but we're here,
and we're listening and taking notes."

And even if they don't trust us yet,
they nod along. Wanting to know
if we'll really stay. Waiting to see
if we will prove ourselves
in the long run.

"Time to play"

Clint says, so we move to the front.
It's not a stage, but we have everyone's
attention. Everyone's eyes on us.

"Welcome to Limestone!" Skye shouts
in the new microphone we bought,
attached to the new sound system.
Figured we might do more of these
potluck concerts. Invite the city.
"Name's Skye. This is James,
Clint, Natalia, and this is . . . Chloe.
She's new. You might not have met her
just yet, but she lives here now.
We all do. And we got some songs
just for y'all."

Clint puts his arm up in the air
so we know it's time to start
and I can feel his skin electric.
I feel like the sunset too,
all full and bursting inside.
And when we start to play
and when we start to sing
and when the light dips
into night, I see us
illuminated.

All That Shines

We take the night.
Our voices
brand-new
together.

They let me in
and I learn
the way.

Mom's face
mimics mine
in the shadows.

I see myself
reflected back
and I love her.

The way she
sparkles, glimmers
all lit up.

Tonight, we are
flashing. Glowing,
gathering.

We don't have a name
just yet, but in my head,
I call us radiant.

Call us brilliant, beacon,

call us sunlight, incandescent,
call us luminous.

Because we are.

ACKNOWLEDGMENTS

It is with steady love that I forever call the names of all the friends &
artists who have guided & shaped me & the stories I tell. Thankful
always for: Grisel Y. Acosta, Stephanie Dionne Acosta, E.J. Antonio,
Lisa Ascalon, Jennifer Baker, Julia Berick, Dan Bernitt, Berry,
Leslie Hibbs Blincoe, Tokumbo Bodunde, Marc Boone, Cheryl
Boyce-Taylor, Lori Brown-Niang, Susan Buttenwieser, Moriah
Carlson, Esther Castillo, Becca Christensen, Cheryl Clarke, Olivia
Cole, Athena Colón, Angie Cruz, LeConté Dill, Wanda Dingman,
Mitchell L. H. Douglas, Jason Duchin, Dana Edell, Kelly Norman
Ellis, John Ellrodt, Kathy Engel, Maria Fico, Rajeeyah Finnie-
Myers, D.A. Flores, Kevin Flores, Marsha Flores, DuEwa Frazier,
Asha French, Tanya Gallo, Catrina Ganey, Megan Clark Garriga,
Sandralis Gines-Gonzalez, Aracelis Girmay, Ysabel Y. Gonzalez,
Nanya-Akuki Goodrich, Lisa Green, Andrée Greene, Rachel Eliza
Griffiths, Jake Hagan, Jen Hagan, Lisa Hagan, Michael Hagan,
Karen Harryman, Lindsey Homra, JP Howard, Melissa Johnson,
Amanda Johnston, Parneshia Jones, Carey Kasten, Caroline Kennedy,
Michele Kotler, Britt Kulsveen, Nikita Ladd, Rob Linné, Veronica
Liu, Mino Lora, Tim Lord, Will Maloney, Alison McDonald, Caits
Meissner, Stacy Mohammed, Yesenia Montilla, Andrea Murphy,
Christina Olivares, Willie Perdomo, Andy Powell, Sarina Prabasi,
Danni Quintos, Emily Raboteau, David Reilly, Carla Repice, Brandi
Cusick Rimpsey, Lisa Forsee Roby, Kate Dworkoski Scudese, Pete

Scudese, Melanie Ballard Sewell, Kate Carothers Smith, Vincent
Toro, Natalia Torres, Alondra Uribe, Jessica Wahlstrom, Renée
Watson, Jenisha Watts, Kelly Wheatley, Alecia Whitaker, Crystal
Wilkinson & Marina Hope Wilson.

In loving memory of Miriam Dawson Hagan and William Paul
Hagan. You built so much of my love for Kentucky right there in your
New Haven home & backyard.

Thank you to my early & brilliant readers: Renée Watson & Kelly
Wheatley—thank you for your thoughtfulness, your tenderness, your
beautiful ways of seeing stories.

Thank you to Jeff Östberg, who made Kentucky & young love
look so stunning & true on the cover.

Thank you, Sarah Shumway Liu— For seeing this journey of self,
for finding the poems that sing, for helping me to make music & love
stories about Kentucky come alive.

Thank you to the truly awesome team at Bloomsbury: Erica
Barmash, Alexa Higbee, Beth Eller & Lily Yengle, Diane Aronson,
Jill Freshney, Nick Sweeney, Kei Nakatsuka, and Hannah Rivera—
for all the work you do to get our books ushered into the world.

So much love to Artavia Jarvis, Lilliam Rivera & Jeff Zentner
for your beautiful words & helping to usher this book into the
world.

Rosemary Stimola— You & your team are such stars! You help
us shine, shine! Shout-out to everyone at Stimola Literary Studio,
especially Allison Hellegers, Erica Rand Silverman & Adriana
Stimola for your support & love.

For the collectives that helped to raise me as a writer & educator
& activist: the Affrilachian Poets, Alice Hoffman Young Writers
Retreat at Adelphi University, Café Buunni, Conjwoman, the
DreamYard Project, Dodge Poetry Festival, Elma's Heart Circle,
girlstory, GlobalWrites, International Poetry Exchange Program,
Kentucky Governor's School for the Arts, New York Foundation
for the Arts, Northern Manhattan Arts Alliance, Northwestern

University Press, People's Theatre Project, Sawyer House Press, Spalding University MFA program, and VONA.

Thank you, Gianina & Patrick Hagan, for always hosting the best parties, for always opening your doors. For teaching me how to love.

Thank you, David Flores. I love you always! Exclamation mark kind of love. Thank you for the everlasting. For always saying yes. For your artist vision, for being home to me.

Thank you, Araceli & Miriam Flores. Oh, how I love the way you two are shining & blooming right in front of me. I stand in forever awe of you both.

This book is about family. Both the ones you are born into & the ones you find. Thank you always to the house party, the block party, the community meetup, the town hall, the potluck, the y'all come back now, the open door, the invitation, the deep love of gathering & being together. Thank you all for always coming over & always with such love.